Mango Digger

A Mango Bob and Walker Adventure

by

Bill Myers

www.mangobob.com

Mango Digger by Bill H. Myers

ISBN-10:1987704479
ISBN-13: 978-1987704471

Version 2018.15.04

Chapter One

She wanted me to call her Paige. Paige Mendoza. Her real name was Abigail. Abigail L. Turner. I never did find out what the L. stood for. She wouldn't tell me. Said it didn't matter. Said to call her Paige. Not Abigail, not Abby. Just Paige.

She'd shown up with Devin three hours earlier. A surprise because Devin was to come alone. No one else was supposed to be with her.

But apparently, plans had changed. Abigail, aka Paige, would be going in Devin's place. No one asked me if that'd be okay. If they had, they would have learned it wasn't. I wasn't happy with the change.

I could put up with Devin even though she was a real pain. We'd spent a week on the road together before and I knew what to expect with her. But I didn't know anything about this Paige or Abigail or whatever her name was. She was a total stranger.

We'd be forced to live together in the tight quarters of my motorhome for a week while traveling more than two thousand miles. If she got on my nerves or I got on hers, it'd make for a miserable trip. I wanted to tell Devin, "No." No change in plans.

But she wouldn't let me. She wouldn't stop talking about her replacement and the more I heard about the new girl the more I knew the trip was going to be a disaster.

I finally got a word in edgewise. "She's a goat girl? Are you telling me I'm going to be spending a week on the road with a goat girl?"

Devin shook her head. "No, Walker, that's not what I said. She's not a goat girl. It's just that she's shy and when she gets nervous, she tends to faint. Kind of like the fainting goats you see on TV. Other than that, she's pretty normal—most of the time. And she's not a little girl. She's a grown woman about your age."

Devin had shown up an hour before dawn, just like we'd planned. She was supposed to be packed and ready to go. We had a long drive ahead and needed to get on the road early to avoid morning rush hour traffic through Tampa.

The first thing she had said when she stepped into my motorhome was, "There's been a slight change in plans. I'm not going with you. The new girl is."

Like I said, no one bothered to tell me and I wasn't happy with the change.

"So, you're not going, and I'll be spending seven days on the road with a goat girl? Whose idea was that? Yours? And why a replacement? Why not just let me do this on my own?"

Kat, a mutual friend, had been missing for three days. She'd parked her new motorhome in a small campground in Arkansas and had overstayed her reservation. The campground manager, wanting to free up the site and concerned about the missing woman, called the emergency contact number on Kat's reservation form.

The call went to Boris Chesnokov, Kat's father, former Don of South Florida's Russian Mob. When he learned his daughter was missing, he called Devin—his 'go to' girl for missions involving his grown daughter.

In a way that only a Mafia boss can, he asked Devin to get me to go with her to find Kat. It was a request she couldn't turn down.

Boris knew me from work I'd done for him before, a job that involved finding out who had hacked into his computer network and security system. Most of what I had done for him had been legal. Some of it might have strayed into a legal gray area; not saying it did, but it could have.

I found the culprit, shut down his operation and everyone was happy, except for the hacker. He was taken away in cuffs by the FBI. No one is quite sure where they took him.

Boris was quite appreciative and paid me well. He suggested there would be opportunities to work together in the future, a suggestion that might have sounded like a threat to some, but not to me.

Before he brought me on board for the first job, Boris had thoroughly checked me out. He knew where I grew up, where I went to school, about my time in the service, and the jobs I'd held since. He also knew I was unemployed, lived in a motorhome and somehow had enough money stashed away that I didn't need to work for a living.

So when he got the call from the campground manager in Arkansas about his daughter, he knew from his research that I had grown up in the area where she had gone missing. He figured my local knowledge would give me a better chance of finding her than the other people he could send. He told Devin to bring me on board. I was 'volunteered' for the job.

I understood why he wanted me, but wasn't sure why he wanted Devin to go. I didn't need her help and having a woman living with me in the motorhome would complicate matters when it came to bathroom time and sleeping arrangements.

That's because my motorhome is not that big. It's certainly not one of those rolling palaces you see the rich and famous driving. Mine is a Class C, the size of a small UPS truck. It has a bedroom in the back with a tiny bathroom across from it, a small kitchen amidships, and a couch up front. I sleep in the bed on the back. And guests, when I have them, sleep on the fold out couch. Or they try to. The couch, with its hard cushions and seam down the middle, isn't very comfortable.

But it wouldn't matter whether the couch was comfortable or not if I went alone because no one would need to sleep on it. I could have the whole place to myself and there'd be no need to try to play nice with a stranger.

I let Devin know how I felt.

"Devin, if you're not going, there's no need for the goat girl to tag along. I can do it on my own. It'll be better that way, no one to slow me down or get in my way.

"So as soon as the goat girl shows up, you can tell her to go back home. I don't need her."

Devin put a finger to her lips and whispered, "Walker, lower your voice. She's out in the car and she's probably listening. It'll hurt her feelings if she hears you call her a goat girl."

I lowered my voice. "You left her out in the car? Why'd you do that? Why didn't you bring her in with you?"

"I already told you. She's shy. She didn't want to come in until I told you about her. She doesn't like change and didn't think you would either.

"If she had her way, she wouldn't be going on this trip. She'd be back home writing poetry or whatever it is she does in her spare time. She sure wouldn't be dreaming about

6

spending time cooped up in a motorhome with the likes of you."

I started to object to the "likes of me" comment but decided against it. Instead, I said, "Good. She doesn't want to go. Fine. Send her home."

Devin frowned. "I can't do that. You have to take her. Boris said so. He's the one who wants her to go instead of me. If you have a problem with that, call him."

She reached into her pocket, pulled out her phone and held it out to me. "Go ahead. Call him. But before you do, you'll want to know that Boris thinks very highly of this woman. He says she has a gift. One that can help find his daughter.

"He might not be happy if you refuse to take her with you. But it's up to you. If you don't mind making him mad, go ahead, call him. He's number four on my speed dial."

She held out the phone, waiting for me to take it.

She knew I wouldn't make the call, but she wasn't going to let me off the hook. She raised her eyebrows and asked, "You going to call him? You going to tell him you're not going to take the woman he personally chose to help you find his daughter?"

There was only one answer to that question and Devin knew it. I wasn't going to call Boris. No way.

It wasn't that I was afraid of him. He had been fair to me in the past and I sensed he would be fair to me in the future. But that might change if I didn't take the goat girl and failed to find his daughter.

When I didn't answer Devin's question, she put the phone back in her pocket and pulled out a thick, white envelope. It was stuffed with hundred-dollar bills, a credit card and a sheet of paper with printing on it.

"Boris said to give you this. He said to use the credit card to pay for gas and hotels. Use the cash to cover everything else. Keep what's left."

Instead of taking the envelope, I asked, "What's her name?"

Chapter Two

"Abigail. That's her name. You'll like her once you get to know her. All you have to do is be nice."

I nodded. "I can be nice. What's her gift?"

"What do you mean?"

"You said she had a gift, something that was supposed to help me find Kat. What kind of gift does she have?"

Devin shrugged. "I don't know. Boris said she had a gift. He didn't tell me what it was and I didn't ask. But if you want to know, call him. "

She pretended to reach for her phone again but stopped before pulling it out. She knew I wasn't going to make the call.

I scratched my head and said, "No need to bother him this early in the morning. He's probably still asleep."

Devin smiled. "Yeah, you don't want to wake him. I'm sure that's the only reason you don't want to call."

She was starting to get on my nerves. Maybe it was good she wasn't going with me. I didn't need her nonstop snarkiness for the next seven days.

I decided to be the better person and said, "I hope her gift is not mind reading because she wouldn't be happy reading mine right now."

Devin laughed. "Yeah, I think you'd be in a lot of trouble around a woman who could read your mind. Nothing good could come of that.

"Still, being able to read minds? That'd make my job a lot easier. Call me if you find out she can. I'll put her to work."

I wasn't sure what Devin meant when she said it would make her job a lot easier. As far as I knew, she'd never held a real job. She was a professional con artist. That's what she did for a living. Con people out of money, valuables and time.

When I'd first met Devin, Kat had called her the "queen of the long con". She said I should be real careful around her and not to believe anything she said. If I had listened to her, it would have saved me a lot of grief. Devin conned me big time. I had bruises and an empty wallet to prove it.

Rather than bring this up, I took a deep breath and kept my mouth shut. I knew that instead of standing around arguing with her, I needed to get on the road and head to the last place Kat had been seen—a campsite twelve hundred miles north at a remote crystal mine in Arkansas, just north of Hot Springs National Park.

I nodded toward the door. "Go get her. Time's a wasting and we have a long way to go."

Devin smiled, but instead of reaching for the door she said, "Walker, before I bring her in here, there are a few things you need to know.

"Like I said, she's shy. She may not talk much until she feels comfortable around you. Whatever you do, don't raise your voice when you're speaking to her. Don't let anyone else raise their voice around her either."

I nodded. That wouldn't be a problem. I don't raise my voice much. Don't need to.

She continued. "Don't let her get drunk. She doesn't hold her liquor well. Don't lose her in a crowd; you'll never find her again. Don't let her gamble. She'll lose all your money. And whatever you do, don't sleep with her. Got it?"

I smiled and tried to make a joke, "She's not going to be much fun is she? No yelling, no drinking, no gambling and no sleeping with the goat girl."

Devin didn't laugh. Instead, she punched me on the shoulder. "Don't call her a goat girl. It's not funny."

She turned and went out to her car.

While I waited, I wondered what I was getting into. I'd be traveling with a stranger, one that had come with a set of rules, and, supposedly, some kind of 'gift'.

I was half tempted to lock the door, jump in the driver's seat and take off. It would have been easier that way. Just me and the road. No one to bother me or get in my way. I could drive as long as I wanted, stop whenever I liked, and not have to worry about upsetting a goat girl.

I reached in my pocket for the keys. Maybe leaving without her was for the best. But I hesitated. I heard voices from outside, a whisper between two women.

One of them sounded upset, reluctant to get out of the car. Devin pleaded with her. "Please do this. Boris will be upset with me if you don't."

After a few seconds of silence, the sound of a car door being opened. Then closed. A moment later, Devin opened the door to my motorhome and stepped in, the goat girl close behind.

She stood about five foot three, a little on the skinny side, wearing pajamas covered with little cartoon sheep jumping over fences. A pink stocking cap hid most of her hair. The few curls that had escaped revealed a streak of purple. She had a phone in one hand and the handle of a pink suitcase in the other. The suitcase looked heavy and full.

11

Devin introduced us. "Abigail, this is Walker. He'll be your driver for the next few days."

I smiled at being called her 'driver' and nodded in her direction. She didn't return the smile. Instead, she looked down at the fuzzy bunny slippers on her feet and mumbled something that sounded like, "Seepy."

She looked toward the back of the motorhome and then back at me. I could see my reflection in her mirrored sunglasses, and I didn't look happy.

She set her suitcase on the floor and, in a soft voice, asked, "Where's the cat?"

I wasn't surprised she knew about my cat. Devin had probably warned her there was one living in the motorhome with me. Some people are allergic to cats and others are afraid of them. If Abigail was either, she wasn't going to be happy when she saw mine.

His name is Mango Bob, and he's big, almost twenty pounds of muscle and fur and still growing every day. An orange tabby, born with just a stub of a tail, pointy ears and raised hind quarters. In the wild, people would mistake him for a bobcat. He has the look. And the attitude.

But he doesn't live in the wild. He lives in the motorhome with me.

I pointed to the bedroom. "Back there, on the bed."

She nodded, grabbed her suitcase and headed to the back. She stepped into my bedroom, pulled her suitcase in behind her and closed the door. The sound of the lock being set was unmistakable.

I turned to Devin. "What does she think she's doing? She went into my bedroom and locked the door?"

. Devin nodded. "Yeah, she does things like that. But

don't worry, she'll be fine. She likes cats."

I wasn't worried about the cat. Bob can take care of himself. He's proven that many times over. I was more worried about a strange woman going into my bedroom, locking the door and going through my things.

Devin let it pass. She reached into her pocket and pulled out the cash-filled envelope. "Take the money. Use the credit card for fuel, and follow the route marked on the map."

"What map?"

She nodded toward the envelope. "In there."

I took the envelope and saw a folded sheet of paper in between the hundred-dollar bills. I pulled it out and shoved the envelope with the cash into my pocket. I didn't need the money, but if Boris wanted me to have it, I wasn't going to turn it down.

Unfolding the paper, I saw that someone had created a custom route on a Google map with little pushpin icons showing places to stop.

I shook my head. "I don't need this. I know the way and this isn't it."

Devin nodded toward the back bedroom. "Abigail made it. She says it's the route Kat took and the places she stopped. She wants you to go the same way, stop at the same places and camp in the same campgrounds. She said it'll help her find Kat."

I looked at the map again. It showed us getting on I-75, going north around Sarasota and Tampa and staying on the interstate all the way to Mobile. Then up through Hattiesburg and on to Jackson, Mississippi and Vicksburg, where we were to spend the night at the Ameristar Casino RV park.

"She wants us to do all this in a day? That's eight hundred miles. Maybe we could do it in a car, but in a motorhome? No way. Even if we don't run into traffic or weather, it'll take us at least fifteen hours."

Devin smiled. "Yeah, it's going to be a long drive. You probably ought to get started."

She headed for the door but stopped before going out. She turned and said, "I put your number on Abigail's phone. She might text you while you're driving. Try not to wreck when you read them."

She smiled and said, "Have fun."

She stepped out of the motorhome, walked over to her car, and drove off, leaving me, Bob and the goat girl behind.

Chapter Three

I thought about going back and making sure the goat girl was okay, but since she'd locked the bedroom door, I figured she wanted privacy, so I left her alone.

Still, I didn't want to drive off without letting her know we were leaving. We would be going over some rough roads before we hit the highway and, if she wasn't ready, she could bounce off the bed. Maybe get hurt.

So, after starting the motorhome, I went back and stood in front of the bedroom door. Remembering Devin's warning about not raising my voice, I tapped lightly and whispered, "We're getting ready to leave. Be careful in there."

There was no response. I shrugged and went back up front. I took my seat behind the wheel and just as I was about to put the motorhome in gear, my phone buzzed with a text. The sender name was Abigail. The message said, "Follow the map. GG."

I knew what she meant by "follow the map." She wanted me to stick to the route she'd come up with, the one on the printout. She wanted me to follow Kat's path, drive the same roads and stop at the same places.

I could see the logic. But it wasn't the route I would have taken if I were driving to Arkansas. Kat had stayed on the interstate most of the way, avoiding back roads. I would have done the opposite, stuck to the back roads and avoided the interstates.

Still, if Abigail wanted me to follow the map she made, I would. But the other part of the message had me stumped. The two letters at the end. GG.

I knew people used abbreviations when sending texts. Things like LOL or AFAIK or ROTFL. But I didn't know what GG meant.

Then it came to me. GG was an abbreviation for Goat Girl. Maybe she had overheard Devin and me talking about her. If she had, maybe she didn't mind being called a goat girl or maybe she had a sense of humor.

I sure hoped so. She'd need it on this trip.

The night before, I had gotten the motorhome ready for the road. I'd topped off the fuel, checked the air in the tires, filled the fresh water and dumped the gray and black tanks. I'd unhooked from shore power before Devin arrived and made sure everything was stowed away.

I'd been living in the motorhome for almost a year, ever since I lost my job and needed a place to stay. I wasn't looking for a motorhome when I was trying to find a place to live, but it was for sale and the price was right. I bought it, moved in, and planned my first trip.

A friend suggested I go to Florida. She said her sister lived there near the beach, and I could live in my motorhome in her back yard. The only catch was I had to pick up a cat in Arkansas and deliver it to the sister in Florida.

It seemed like a fair trade. Drive a thousand miles to Florida in my motorhome with a cat. No big deal, right?

I was wrong. It *was* a big deal.

The cat wasn't happy to be in the motorhome, especially with a stranger. He preferred life in a home that wasn't moving down the road at sixty miles an hour, bouncing up and down with every bump.

He tried to escape every time I opened the door and almost succeeded once. Long story short, we made it to Florida. I delivered the cat, Mango Bob, to the woman's sister as promised and lived in my motorhome in her backyard until she changed jobs and needed to move.

Her new place didn't allow cats and she asked me to keep Bob until she sorted things out. I reluctantly agreed, figuring it would only be a week or so before she came back to get him.

But she never did come back. She never returned my calls or texts, and eventually changed her number. After nine months, I figured she wasn't coming back and I was stuck with the cat. And he was stuck with me.

I was still sitting in the driver's seat, thinking about this and letting the motorhome warm up, when my phone buzzed again with an incoming text. The message said, "What are you waiting for? Drive! GG."

The goat girl was right; I needed to get on the road. We had a long way to go before we could pack it in for the day. I rechecked her map and saw our first scheduled stop was two hundred fifty miles north, just past Tallahassee at the Pilot Travel Center.

I put the map away, put the motorhome in gear, and headed out.

Chapter Four

Even though I had wasted time arguing with Devin about the change of plans, we'd still managed to get on the road an hour before sun up. Leaving early was the only way to avoid morning rush hour traffic around Tampa. If you didn't get by before it jammed up, you could be stuck for hours.

Leaving my site at Mango Bay in Englewood, I drove the mostly deserted side streets that would lead me out onto I-75. There weren't many other people on the roads and I made good time. As soon as I got on the interstate, I set the cruise control to sixty-five and hugged the right lane.

The speed limit was seventy, but only the timid and those of us in motorhomes were taking it seriously. Everyone else was pushing at least eighty and some were doing ten over that. It was like a game of chicken. The fastest drivers, those leading the pack, would get there first, but only if they didn't get stopped by the highway patrol.

Early morning, the troopers were stretched thin, usually only two or three covering the fifty-mile stretch between Sarasota and Tampa. To make the most of their limited resources, they concentrated their efforts near the construction zones. Armed with radar guns, they looked for the leaders of the pack, those running ninety plus.

It wasn't long before I saw flashing blue lights up ahead. A trooper had pulled over a dark blue BMW that had flown by me earlier. The driver, with a cup of coffee in his hand, must have been doing at least eighty-five, maybe ninety when he passed me. Now he was doing zero, parked on the side of the road.

It would be an expensive ticket for the driver. In Florida, speeding fines are doubled in construction zones.

I eased over into the middle lane to give the trooper plenty of room and continued on my way. Once I had cleared the blue lights, I moved back into the right lane.

The sun was just starting to break over the horizon when I reached the outskirts of Tampa. It was still an hour before rush hour and traffic was light. Sitting up high in the motorhome, I could see a clear path ahead with nothing to slow me down, a rare sight on the roads around Tampa.

I knew if I could get past the I-4 junction, the main artery that led to Orlando and Disney to the east, it'd be smooth sailing to Tallahassee. No big cities or traffic jams to slow me down after that.

Getting through Tampa without problems meant we might be able to make Vicksburg before the end of the day. With clear roads as far as I could see, I bumped the cruise control up to seventy and settled in for the long, boring drive ahead.

Normally, Mango Bob would be in the passenger seat beside me. I'd talk to him as I drove, pointing out things he'd be interested in. Big trucks carrying cows or horses were his favorites. He'd sit up and make huffing sounds when the animal smells reached him. But most of the time, he'd just lie in the passenger seat and sleep.

Today the passenger seat was empty. Bob was in the back with the goat girl, leaving me all alone up front.

Three hours and two hundred miles later, my phone buzzed with a text message. Normally, I would have ignored it, as I'm not one of those people who gets a lot of texts, and

I usually don't check them while driving. But Devin had told me that Abigail might text and, frankly, I was interested in what she had to say.

Plus, I was bored.

The interstates through Florida are mostly flat and straight. No mountains in the distance, no majestic scenery to stimulate your senses. Just green grass, palm trees and pavement. With no traffic around, I figured it'd be safe to check my phone.

I pulled it out, swiped the screen and looked at the message. It said, "GG bored. Coming up front."

Just like before, she had referred to herself as GG. Goat Girl. Maybe she did have a sense of humor. That would be good. I texted back, "OK."

A few moments later, I heard the bedroom door open followed by the pitter patter of Bob's footsteps. He went into the bathroom to use the litter box and after taking care of business, he came up front to join me. He hopped onto the passenger seat and said, "Murrrph." Then began to clean himself.

From the back of the motorhome, I heard the toilet flush, followed by the sound of running water in the sink. Looking up at the rear-view mirror, I saw Abigail come out of the bathroom, heading in my direction.

She had changed out of her pajamas into skin-tight, black yoga pants and a clingy, white top. No longer wearing a knit cap, her auburn hair flowed onto her bare shoulders. No sign of the purple streak. She must have washed it out.

She was still wearing her mirrored sunglasses and from a distance, she looked a lot like Danica Patrick of NASCAR fame. She had the 'look' and definitely wasn't a goat girl.

While trying to keep an eye on the road ahead, I kept

glancing up at the mirror to see what she was doing. I expected her to come up front and take the passenger seat. But if that was her plan, she wasn't in any hurry.

Instead, she stopped and touched each surface of the motorhome as she passed. Eyes closed, slowly moving her hands, feeling the textures. First the kitchen counter, then the kitchen cabinets, then the stove and finally the fridge.

It looked like something out of a séance, as though she expected the appliances to send her some kind of message. I couldn't imagine what the counter or stove might be telling her, maybe something about needing to be cleaned.

With both hands flat on the fridge door, she slowly turned her head, opened her eyes and looked in my direction. She caught me watching her and shook her head like I'd done something wrong.

I tried my best not to look. But it was hard not to, seeing her strange behavior while trying to figure out what the heck she was doing with her hands. I wanted to watch non stop, but I couldn't. I had to keep my eyes on the road. We were doing seventy and I didn't want to take too many chances. Still, I wanted to see what she was doing.

I glanced up at the mirror again. She was still at the fridge but her eyes were no longer closed. Now they were watching me. I quickly returned my focus to the road, but it was too late. From behind me, I heard her say, "I saw you looking."

Her breathy voice surprised me. Sultry, almost sexy, and I wanted to hear more, so I said, "I couldn't help myself."

She smiled just slightly and said, "I know."

Chapter Five

She opened the fridge, pulled out two bottles of water and brought them up front. Bob heard her coming and jumped down out of the passenger seat. He trotted over to her and leaned against her ankle as she passed. Then he jumped up on the couch and curled up for a nap.

Abigail took the passenger seat and turned to me. "I brought you a water."

I was thirsty and had been thinking about water since before she texted me about coming up front. I'd even considered texting back and asking her to grab a bottle on her way up. But I hadn't.

Still, she'd shown up with water, almost like she read my mind. But I knew she couldn't. No one can read minds. At least, that's what the experts say.

The water was cold and felt good going down. I took two long sips, then put the bottle in the cup holder on the dash. When I did, I saw that she had been watching me drink. I smiled and she quickly looked away. She'd been caught watching me, and apparently that embarrassed her. I decided maybe it was a good time to try to start a conversation.

I started with an easy question, something she might feel comfortable talking about.

"So, you like cats. You have one at home?"

She shook her head. "No, not anymore."

She paused then the words started spilling out. "I had a

cat for a long time. His name was Bandit and he was the best cat ever. He went everywhere I went, even slept with me at night. When I'd go places in my car, he'd go along and sit in the passenger seat and meow softly."

She paused, then said, "I really loved Bandit. I miss him so much now that he's gone."

I nodded and wanted to ask what had happened to Bandit. But I didn't because I was pretty sure the answer wouldn't make either of us feel better.

She could either read my mind or decided to answer without being asked. "It was kidney failure. They say it's common with older cats. He was seventeen, and the vet said there was nothing they could do for him.

"I was with him until the end."

The conversation hadn't gone as I'd planned. I had hoped to get her talking about something that made her happy, but instead the subject had dredged up painful memories. The sadness in her voice was apparent. I needed to come up with something else.

Fortunately, Bob came to my rescue. He trotted up front and jumped onto Abigail's lap. Almost instinctively, she began to stroke his back and he began to purr.

We rode like this for another twenty miles. Me driving, Abigail with Bob in her lap, purring. I glanced over and saw that she was smiling. It was a good look for her.

She continued to pet Bob and finally said, "He's a good cat. Does he like riding up front with you?"

I nodded. "Most of the time he does, especially when we're on the highway and there isn't much traffic. He likes to sit there and groom himself to sleep."

She nodded knowingly. "My Bandit loved riding in the

car with me. Whenever I grabbed my keys, he'd come running. He'd go outside and wait at the car door until I opened it. Then he'd jump in and find his place in the passenger seat.

"If we were traveling with friends, they'd all have to ride in the back because Bandit was going to ride up front with me."

I nodded. "Sounds like he was quite a character."

She smiled again. "He was. There'll never be another one like him."

She looked off to her right, outside the motorhome. I was thinking maybe she was going to dab away a tear. But I was wrong. It wasn't a tear that was bothering her. It was something else. She looked over at me and asked, "How long has that white van back there been following us?"

I looked in my side mirror and saw the van she was talking about. A late model white Chevy Express. A windowless cargo van. The kind used by plumbers and electricians.

Most of these would have a business name painted on the side, and below the name, a phone number and maybe the company website. But the van behind us was too far back to tell if it had anything painted on it.

We'd been on the road for more than three hours and not many vehicles stayed behind us for long. We were going slower than most everyone else and not many people wanted to be behind us. They couldn't see over or around us and knew that if traffic slowed or merged into a single lane, they'd be stuck, so they usually passed us as soon as they could.

I hadn't noticed the white van earlier. But there was no reason to suspect that it or any other vehicle would be following us. And the van hadn't done anything that made it suspicious. It was just another of the thousands of cars, trucks, and RVs traveling west on Florida's Interstate 10.

Abigail asked, "Do you see the one I'm talking about? The white van? Back there in the right lane? How long has it been following us?"

I checked the side mirror again and could see the van was still behind us, maintaining its distance. Not getting any closer, not falling back. That in itself wasn't unusual. I had my cruise control set to the posted speed limit of seventy. If the van's driver had set his to seventy, he would be matching our speed and wouldn't be gaining on us or losing ground.

I didn't want to explain all of this to Abigail, so I just said, "I see him. You think he's following us?"

She nodded. "He's behind us, so he's definitely following us. I just don't know if he is following *us* or is just another traveler on the road."

I couldn't argue with her logic, so I said nothing.

She continued to watch the side mirror, checking on the white van. After a few minutes, it sped up and passed us on the left. It had the words "Unlimited Plumbing and Drain Service" painted on its side. Below the name, a street address in Perry, Florida.

Two ladders were strapped to the roof and, as it passed us, we could see plumbing supplies inside on metal racks.

Wanting to see what Abigail thought, I asked, "So what do you think? Was it following us?"

She smiled. "No, I don't think it was after us. I was just being paranoid. There's no reason for anyone to be following us, right?"

I wasn't sure why she was asking me. I couldn't think of

any reason for anyone to be following us or to even care what we were doing. As far as the rest of the world knew, we were just two people and a cat in a motorhome traveling across Florida. Nothing unusual about that.

Still, I felt a need to answer her question, so I said, "I don't think anyone would be following me. How about you? Any reason someone would be following you?"

She shook her head. "No, not that I can think of. No husbands or boyfriends to worry about. No bill collectors or parole officers either. Maybe it's your ex-wife. Think she has someone checking up on you?"

I hadn't told her about my ex-wife so I was surprised she had asked the question. But the answer was easy. My ex-wife had ended our marriage on good terms. It was her idea, and, as far as she was concerned, there weren't any hard feelings. There'd be no reason she'd have anyone following me.

Still, I wondered how Abigail knew I'd been married, so I asked her about it. "What makes you think I have an ex-wife?"

She smiled, but, instead of answering, she said, "You do, don't you? And no children. Right?"

She was right. There had been no children in our marriage. The ex-wife wanted it that way. Turned out it was for the best.

I nodded. "How'd you know?"

She shrugged. "Just had a feeling. You dating anyone these days?"

In the course of ten minutes, she'd gone from not speaking a word to me since her introduction three hours earlier to asking personal questions and knowing things about me that she shouldn't. The fact that she felt comfortable enough to ask these questions was probably a good sign, but her knowing about my personal life was unnerving.

"No, I'm not dating anyone. And I don't have any husbands, girlfriends or wives following me. Right now, it's just me and Bob. And you."

She smiled, seemingly happy with my answer.

Chapter Six

After listening to her questions about my personal life, I decided that riding in silence wasn't so bad. As far as I was concerned, as long as there were no more questions, I was comfortable with the silence. She seemed to be as well, at least for a while.

Twenty minutes later, she asked, "How long were you married?"

It was yet another question about my personal life, one that I didn't feel like answering. Not that I was ashamed the marriage had ended, I just didn't want to talk about it.

So, instead of answering, I asked, "What did Devin tell you about me?"

She laughed. "Devin? She didn't tell me much. She said you lived in a motorhome and had a cat. When I asked her what you were like, she said that most of the time you were like Clark Kent—easy going, a little shy, happy to let other people take credit.

"But she warned me not to be fooled. She said that like Clark Kent, you had a secret identity. But yours wasn't Superman. She said you were more like the Hulk. Make you mad, and things could go south quickly. She said she didn't believe it at first, but saw it first-hand. Said you took on three guys in a parking lot."

I knew what she was talking about. Three guys beating up a defenseless man and somebody needed to step in and end it. Turned out it was me. I left the three guys on the ground. It wasn't something I was proud of, but it had to be done.

I didn't tell Abigail this. I just said, "I'm not the Hulk, and I'm not Clark Kent. I'm just a regular guy."

She laughed. "Yeah, she said you'd say that. She also said that, like Superman, you had a weakness. Instead of kryptonite, yours was women, especially those that needed help. She said you'd believe anything they told you. You'd do whatever they wanted. Is that true?"

I didn't want to admit it, but it was true. For some reason, I felt compelled to help women in need. Maybe it was the way I was raised. Or maybe it was some of the things I'd seen in Kandahar. Whatever the reason, I was always willing to step in and help if I could.

Sometimes it backfired. I'd believe their stories no matter how farfetched. I'd volunteer to help, even if it meant doing things like driving across country with a stranger—or their cat.

I hesitated with my answer. I didn't want to admit my weakness, especially since Abigail, like Devin before her, could use it to her advantage. So I was relieved when she said, "Don't worry, I've learned not to put too much stock in anything Devin says. She has a history of making things up. You probably know that."

I nodded. "Yeah, I learned about Devin the hard way. She's a big fan of make believe. She fooled me before with her tall tales and will probably fool me again."

Abigail laughed. "I think she already has."

"What do you mean?"

She reached out and touched my arm. "Remember what she said about me this morning while I was outside waiting in the car?"

I nodded. "Yeah, I remember. What about it?"

With a grin, she said, "I could hear most of what she was telling you. And it isn't true. I'm not that shy. I don't faint like a goat. I don't get lost in crowds, and I don't have a drinking or gambling problem."

I hoped she was right, but I wasn't convinced. Maybe Devin had stretched the truth a bit, but I'd already seen the goat girl do some strange things.

I decided to ask her about it. "What about this morning? Devin said you were shy. When she introduced us, you walked away without saying a word. You went to the back and stayed there for three hours. What was that about?"

Abigail turned away from me and looked out the side window. I wasn't sure whether she was going to answer or not. Maybe I had hurt her feelings. Maybe she *was* shy and I'd touched a nerve.

But then she turned toward me and said, "Devin showed up at my place at three in the morning. I was still in my pajamas. Not even close to being awake. She drove me a hundred miles and dropped me off at your motorhome. I was so sleepy I could barely keep my eyes open. When I saw you had a bed in the back, I made a beeline for it. It wasn't that I was shy, I was sleepy. I apologize if you took offense."

I shook my head. "No need to apologize. It was my fault for believing Devin."

Turns out the goat girl wasn't shy. She was just sleepy.

"So, you heard me call you Goat Girl this morning?"

She nodded, "I did. And I thought it was funny. Me, the goat girl."

She put her fingers beside her ears like little horns and said, "Baaaaaaa."

It was weird. And funny. Her "Baaaaa" sounded more like a sheep than a goat. Maybe she didn't know the difference. Maybe she wasn't raised around sheep or goats. Either way, she was strange. No denying that.

She turned to me, stuck her chest out and said, "Maybe I should get a T-shirt with 'Goat Girl' printed on the front. What do you think? Should I?"

I looked to see what she was talking about and immediately forgot the question. Her thrusting chest pose was not what I had expected to see from the Goat Girl. She held it, waiting for my answer. I couldn't think of anything decent to say, so I returned my focus to the road ahead.

"Aren't you going to answer?"

I almost blurted out, "I think you're too pretty to wear a Goat Girl T-shirt," but I knew better than to say that. Too early for that kind of compliment. So I just shrugged and said, "Sure, get a Goat Girl T-shirt if you want. It'll look good on you."

I really didn't care whether she got a Goat Girl shirt or not. If it made her happy, good. I always liked it when women were happy, especially around me.

We rode in silence for another twenty minutes. Then she asked, "How well do you know Kat?"

It was a reasonable question. The only reason we were on the road together was to try to find Kat, assuming she was really missing and not just laying low. Kat was a grown woman and had proven many times over that she could take care of herself. As the daughter of a higher up in the Russian Mafia, she had been trained from an early age in the skills needed to protect herself and deal out punishment when needed.

Kat valued her privacy and I didn't want to go into much

detail about her, so I kept my answer short. "I met her three months ago in Key West. Spent a week with her on the road. Got to know her pretty well. What about you? How well do you know her?"

She was quick with her answer. "Well enough to know she can take care of herself and that she's probably not really missing. Most likely she's having a good time and will be surprised to learn we were sent to find her."

I agreed with her assessment, but I had a question. "Do you know why she was staying at that campground in Arkansas?"

"Yeah, I do. Supposedly she met a guy in Key West. Dylan, I think. He had a table set up at Mallory Square selling what he claimed to be 'healing crystals'.

"Kat was always interested in local con artists, so she struck up a conversation with him and learned he had sold almost all the crystals he had and was getting ready to hitch-hike back to the mines in Arkansas to get more.

"She had been looking for a reason to get out of Key West for a few days and figured taking Dylan to the crystal mine in her motorhome would be as good an excuse as any.

"She asked him if he wanted to go and he said, 'Yes.'

"They left Key West the next day and got to the campground two days later. The manager there said she seemed happy when she registered. He said she paid for three days.

"When her motorhome was still there on the fourth day and she was nowhere to be found, the manager called her emergency contact number, which went to Boris. As soon as he learned she was missing he contacted me.

"I think she's probably off on an adventure and not in any kind of trouble. But just in case, Boris wanted us to go up there to make sure."

Abigail was probably right. Kat was most likely not missing. But it didn't hurt to make sure. Her father did have some powerful enemies, and there was always the chance one of them might see his daughter as a prime target.

We had just reached the eastern edge of Tallahassee, which meant our first stop, the Pilot Flying J Travel Center, was close. A huge billboard announced exit 192 would get us there, just four miles ahead.

When she saw the sign, Abigail said, "I need to go back and change clothes. When you get there, pull up to the pumps and wait for me before you get out."

She headed to the back while I watched for our exit. I didn't know what she was changing into, but whatever it was, it needed to do a better job of hiding her lady parts than the skin-tight yoga pants she was wearing. I personally didn't mind but was worried they might attract a little too much attention at truck stop full of road-weary male drivers.

I took the exit and followed the arrows to the Flying J lot. Pulling in, I saw that there were ten rows of gas pumps; with the one on the far right reserved for motorhomes. I pulled over and took my place in line.

We were third; a Dodge minivan filled with kids was in front of us and a green pickup in front of them. Neither belonged in the motorhome lane, but they probably didn't know any better or couldn't read the sign. Since it looked like it might be a few minutes before we got our turn at the pump, I killed the motor, not wanting to waste gas.

Glancing up at the rear-view mirror, I saw Abigail coming out of my bedroom. She was wearing a white T-shirt with a Doc Ford's Rum Bar logo, faded jean shorts and a Key West Conchs baseball cap.

She saw me looking at her and asked, "So what do you think?"

I wasn't sure what she was asking and didn't know how to answer. My best guess was it had to do with what she was wearing, so I winged it and said, "I like it."

"Good. But do I look like a tourist? Because that's what I'm going for. I want to blend in. I don't want to give anyone a reason to remember us being here."

I looked around the parking lot. It was full of cars, trucks, RVs and eighteen wheelers all wanting the same thing—to get in, fill up with fuel, and get back on the road as quickly as possible. Most didn't have time to take notice of others around them. If they had noticed, they would have seen cowboys, hippies, beach bunnies, soldiers, long-haul truckers and, yes, lots and lots of tourists.

With all the people coming and going, and most only there for a few minutes, even if a person wanted to get noticed, they'd have a hard time at Pilot Flying J—unless they were wearing skin tight yoga pants.

I didn't go into any of this. I just said, "Abigail, if you want to blend in, I'm sure you will."

The truck that was using the pump in front of us pulled away. The minivan pulled into his spot. We were next.

Abigail pointed at my shirt pocket. "You got the credit card in there? The one you're supposed to use for gas?"

I touched my pocket and felt the card. It was still there. I'd pulled it out of the envelope Devin had given me. The cash was still in the envelope, hidden away under my seat.

"Yeah, I've got it."

"Good. When you run it through the pump, use 33050 for the zip code."

I repeated the number. "33050?"

"Yeah, that's it."

She reached into her pocket and pulled out a ring and handed it to me. "Put this on."

It was a gold wedding band.

"You're kidding, right? Why would I want to put on a wedding ring?"

She patted my shoulder like you would a small child. "Humor me. Put it on and wear it while you're pumping gas. I'll tell you why when we get back on the road."

She pulled out another and slipped it on the ring finger of her left hand. She showed it to me, a small diamond mounted on a gold band. She smiled and said, "If anyone asks, we're the Mendozas. You're Tony, and I'm Paige. And we're married."

Before I could think of something to say, she opened the door and walked away.

Chapter Seven

Devin had warned me not to lose Abigail in a crowd. She said I might not ever get her back. But she hadn't warned me about wedding rings.

She should have.

I still had the gold ring in my hand, pretty sure I wasn't going to wear it. It was heavier than I expected. Felt like real gold, maybe even solid gold. If it was, it would have been expensive.

The minivan in front of me pulled away; it was my turn to fill up. I slipped the ring on my finger, started the motorhome and moved up to the pump.

I hopped out and ran the credit card from Boris through the reader. When the screen asked for the zip code, I entered the number Abigail had said to use. It took a few seconds to authorize, but it cleared. I pushed the button for regular, put the nozzle in the fuel fill and set it to automatically shut off when the tank was full.

The motorhome has a fifty-gallon tank and gets about ten miles a gallon. We had traveled just under four hundred miles, and I knew it would take a while for the pump to deliver the fuel we needed.

While waiting for the tank to fill, I walked around and checked the tires. I put my hand on each one, feeling to see if it was hot. If it were, it would mean it needed air.

I had used a gauge to check the air before leaving, but I'd

gotten into the habit of checking again at each stop. In a motorhome, if a tire blew at highway speeds, it could be disastrous, so you checked them often

Fortunately, none of our tires were hot. No air was needed; but I'd check again at each stop along our way. Better safe than sorry.

When I got back to the pump, the display showed twenty gallons in and still going. Knowing I had time to kill, I grabbed the squeegee from the bucket of water next to the gas pump and cleaned the bugs off the motorhome's windshield.

I had just finished when I heard the pump click off. The display showed thirty-eight gallons, pretty much what I expected it would take. I removed the nozzle, replaced the gas cap and locked the filler door.

There were three RVs in line behind me and I didn't want to hold them up needlessly, so I got in the motorhome, started the motor and pulled over to the RV parking area.

After getting parked, I looked around to see if could find Abigail, but she was nowhere in sight. I figured with her out of the motorhome, it would be a good time to use the bathroom, check on Bob, and, if she wasn't back by then, go looking for her.

I was washing my hands when my phone pinged with an incoming text. The message said, "Inside by the deli, bring $$$. GG."

Like most large interstate travel plazas, the Pilot Flying J had a restaurant, a convenience store, and a deli where they made sandwiches to go. Apparently, that's where I'd find Abigail.

I grabbed my wallet and keys, locked up the motorhome and headed across the parking lot, dodging cars heading for the pumps. When I got inside, I saw her standing at the deli checkout and headed in her direction. When she saw me, she smiled and told the clerk at the register, "That's my husband. He's paying for this."

On the counter in front of her were two freshly made sandwiches, a bag of chips, and four cans of Red Bull. The clerk, a young man of Middle Eastern descent, bagged everything up and in a thoroughly American accent, said, "Nineteen dollars and fifty-one cents. Will that be cash or credit?"

I pulled out my wallet and handed the man a twenty. He rang it up and gave me forty-nine cents change. I didn't want to carry a pocket full of coins, so I put them in the collection jar for a local charity next to the register. I grabbed the bag with the sandwiches, and Abigail got the one with the drinks.

When we got outside, I headed to the motorhome and she followed. I was moving pretty fast and Abigail quickly fell a few steps behind. I probably should have waited for her to catch up, but I didn't.

Just as I reached the motorhome, I heard the screech of car tires followed by a loud horn. I turned and saw Abigail standing near the front bumper of an older Ford Focus. It looked like the car had bumped into her, and she was holding the back of her leg, like it might have been hurt.

I ran over and asked, "Are you okay?"

She nodded. "Yeah. I'm fine. She didn't hit me, but she scared the hell out of me when she honked her horn. Her bumper was right on me."

I looked at the driver, a young woman, probably in her early twenties. She had one hand on the wheel, the other holding a phone to her ear. She tapped her horn with her elbow, wanting us to get out of her way.

It was a big parking lot. We had been walking on the far edge, away from most cars. There was no reason for the woman to have gotten that close to Abigail—unless she wasn't paying attention.

On a normal day, I would have gone over and had a talk with her. I would have explained why running over a woman in a parking lot while on the phone wasn't a good idea. I'd also explain how honking a horn at someone after almost hitting them wasn't the best way to handle things. I might even have gone so far as to use my boot to leave a reminder on the driver's door. Maybe it would help her remember to pay attention when behind the wheel. But I didn't do any of that.

It wasn't a normal day. I wasn't alone, and we couldn't waste time giving driving lessons to strangers in a gas station parking lot. So I just waved the driver around, shaking my head in disgust. The important thing was Abigail was uninjured.

When we got back to the motorhome, I opened the side door and helped her in. I guided her to the couch and eased her onto the cushion. She wasn't hurt and didn't need my help, but, for some reason, I felt compelled to treat her as if she were.

I asked again, "Are you sure you're okay?"

She nodded. "I'm fine. Don't worry about it."

She pointed to the bags from the deli. "I bought us lunch. Turkey sandwiches, chips, and cookies. You ready to eat?"

I was.

Chapter Eight

After finishing our sandwiches, I started the motorhome and got us back on the highway. According to Abigail's map, our next stop would be the Love's truck stop, just outside of Mobile, Alabama. About three hours away if all went well.

Abigail wanted to rest in the back while I drove, so I didn't get a chance to ask her about the wedding rings. I also wanted to ask her how she knew Kat, the woman we were supposed to find. I was pretty sure her answers would be interesting.

I set the cruise control to seventy, and without any major cities in front of us, I was pretty sure we'd make good time. Interstate 10 from Tallahassee to Mobile is a straight shot. No city traffic to slow us down, no mountains to climb, just a wide, flat, divided highway bordered on both sides by pine forests.

The only danger the road presented was boredom.

Three hours and two hundred miles later, the energy drink I'd been nursing had made its way well past my bladder and was calling for a pit stop. Abigail hadn't included any 'nature calls' pit stops on her map, but that was her problem; mine was finding a place to pull over in time.

I was twenty miles past the last of the Pensacola exits when I saw a sign that said, "Welcome to Alabama," and just beyond it the exit for the Alabama Welcome Center. Relief was in sight.

I hit the right turn signal, lifted off the gas and let the motorhome burn off speed as we approached the rest area exit. Pulling in, I saw the designated parking area for RVs and headed over to it.

Before I could get parked, Abigail came up from the back and asked, "Why are we stopping? This isn't on the map."

I pulled into a parking spot, killed the motor, and said, "I have to pee." Then, instead of heading back to the bathroom in the motorhome, I got out, walked across the parking lot and used the men's room in the rest area.

It was clean and wasn't crowded, and the walk over gave me a chance to stretch my legs. When I got back inside the motorhome, Abigail was waiting for me. She had moved to the passenger seat and was checking what looked like a copy of the map I'd been given.

She said, "Love's Truck Stop, twenty miles ahead. That's our next stop."

I nodded, started the motor and pulled back out onto I-10. After getting the beast up to cruising speed, I pointed to the ring on my finger and asked, "Why do you want me to wear this?"

She smiled and held up her left hand showing her ring. "So people will think we're married."

I nodded. "And why is that important?"

She didn't answer right away, but after a few seconds of silence, she asked, "When you were married, didn't you feel safe?"

I hadn't thought about it like that, but I did feel safe when I was married. It was like being on a team where the other person had your back. Rather than explain this to her, I just said, "Yeah, I guess I felt safe."

She smiled. "Good. That's why I want you to wear the ring while we're together. It'll make me feel safer knowing you have it on. Like we're connected in some way. And maybe it'll keep women from throwing themselves at you. They'll see the ring and know you're taken."

I wasn't sure whether she was kidding or not. I didn't have a problem with women throwing themselves at me. Sure, strange women would smile from a distance and sometimes come up and talk. I figured they were just being friendly. Maybe I was wrong. Even so, I couldn't see how wearing a ring would change that.

Still, if my wearing the ring meant she felt safer while we were on the road together, I would wear it.

I was still thinking about the ring when I saw the giant sign towering above the highway announcing the location of the Love's truck stop. It was the next exit on our right.

I lifted off the gas, hit the turn signal, and made our way into the Love's lot. With twelve fuel islands to choose from, I pulled up to the one on the far right. I grabbed the keys out of the ignition and before stepping out to pump gas, I asked Abigail if she needed anything. She shrugged. "Won't know until I go inside and see what they have. If I'm not back when you get done, come looking for me."

She opened her door and got out. I watched as she walked across the lot and made sure she got inside safely. Then I stepped out, ran the credit card and started pumping gas.

As before, it took several minutes to fill the tank, and while I waited, I cleaned the windshield, checked the tires, and kept watching for Abigail. After seeing her almost get hit by a car at the last stop, I wanted to be sure she got back in safely.

About the time the gas pump clicked off, she showed up carrying two large shopping bags and a big smile. I opened the door for her and she went inside while I finished up with the pump. When I was done, I went in and headed to the back to try to wash the smell of gas off my hands.

That's when I noticed the door to my bedroom was just slightly open. Looking inside, I saw Bob on the bed, sleeping. Then I noticed the curtains.

Apparently, Abigail had decided to spruce up the place by hanging new curtains over the plain beige ones that had come with the motorhome. The ones she'd put up were bright white and covered with large pink flamingos.

Looking around, I saw the curtains weren't the only thing she'd changed. She'd put a lace doily on the nightstand and had placed a pink flamingo alarm clock in the middle. And she'd emptied the clothes from her suitcase and hung them in my closet. It looked like she was moving in.

I went back up front and asked her, "Where'd you get the curtains?"

She smiled. "You like? The room needed something, and when I saw the flamingo scarves back at the Flying J, I knew they would be perfect."

I nodded. There wasn't much I could say about it. The curtains did liven the place up a bit, but I wondered if she would be doing a full makeover of the motorhome while we were together. I was afraid the bedroom was just the first step.

Still, it wasn't something I had time to worry about. We had miles to go before we could park it for the day. So with Abigail safely back in the motorhome, I started the motor, and we got back on I-10, headed toward Mobile.

Chapter Nine

It was just after three in the afternoon when we reached the Mobile causeway, the seven-mile bridge that spans Mobile Bay. Being just a few feet above sea water at high tide, driving across the causeway with waves lapping at the edges always creates a sense of danger. Add in the steady cross winds coming off the gulf, and driving the causeway in a motorhome can be a challenge.

The posted speed limit is fifty-five, but most everyone in the left lane ignores it. Impatient motorists jump from lane to lane, trying to get ahead of anyone in front of them. But if they jump too far and too fast in either direction, they could go up and over the concrete barrier that separates the causeway from the open waters below.

Knowing this, I stayed in the right lane and kept a safe distance from the truck in front of us.

Signs near the end of the causeway warned of the long tunnel that goes under the bay and comes up near downtown Mobile. The posted speed limit for the tunnel is forty; a flashing light at the entrance warns if you are going too fast. Almost everyone is. The light flashes continually.

I'd been through the tunnel before and knew what to expect. Cars coming up out of the tunnel onto the interstate usually had to suddenly slow down due to traffic congestion. If you were going too fast trying to make the tunnel's uphill run and didn't know about the slowing traffic ahead, you could easily rear end cars stalled in front of you.

Rather than risk it, I kept a steady pace and wasn't tempted to speed up near the end of the tunnel. Drivers behind me didn't like it, but that was their problem. Abigail sensed the potential danger and didn't distract me with questions or conversations until we were safely on the other side. As expected, traffic outside the tunnel was heavy; it had slowed quickly, and two cars that had crashed were on the side. Others would most likely soon join them.

Traffic continued to be heavy as we made our way on I-10 and then onto I-65 to get around Mobile. Cars were darting from lane to lane, most going ten to fifteen miles over the limit. We stayed in the right lane, trying to stay out of everyone's way.

Abigail pretended to be busy, checking her map and shaking her head as cars shot past us. It wasn't until we had gotten off the interstate and onto US 98 north that she spoke again. She sounded relieved when she said, "Glad we didn't have to do that during rush hour."

I nodded. "Yeah, it'd be bad, especially in a motorhome. We'll have to remember that on the way back."

We rode in silence for a few minutes then Abigail stood and said, "I need to go get something from the back."

Without waiting for me to reply, she carefully made her way back to the bedroom, trying to keep her balance with the movement of the swaying motorhome.

A few minutes later, she returned holding a small package. She took her seat, looked over at me and said, "Two things. First, I tried Kat's phone again. Still nothing. Goes straight to voice mail. I've texted and called all day and she hasn't got back to me. So either she forgot to take her phone with her or the battery is dead."

I could think of another possibility, one that involved

foul play, but decided not to bring it up.

She continued, "I'll keep trying her. Maybe she'll eventually pick up."

She took a deep breath and showed me the package she had brought up front. She said, "And second, I bought you something. I hope you like it."

Going north from Mobile, we had left the interstate and the flat wide roads of Florida behind. We had jumped on US 98 and immediately started gaining altitude. The road was four lanes as it made its way through the small town of Semmes, but a few miles later it had narrowed just beyond the bridge at Moffet. From there on, it was a narrow two-lane blacktop with no shoulder. Drop a tire off the edge and you'd be in trouble.

Unlike the interstate, there were no exit or entrance ramps to safely get on or off the road. Cars in front would suddenly slow, often coming to a near stop before turning onto a side road. Cars on side roads would often pull out directly in front of us, playing a game of chicken, gambling that either they could speed up enough to get out of our way or we'd slow down before we ran over them. It was a bet where there'd be two losers if things didn't go right.

The motorhome was carrying more than ten thousand pounds of momentum and it took a lot of effort to get it stopped. That, along with the lack of pullouts and passing lanes and the aging blacktop, made driving through this part of Mississippi a challenge.

I was trying to pay attention to the road when Abigail had said she had bought me something. I glanced over at the package, smiled, and said, "What you'd get?"

She held the package out and said, "Open it, you'll see."

I shook my head. "I can't right now. I kinda need to watch

the road. Will you open it for me?"

She sighed, showing her disappointment. I felt bad that I couldn't open her gift, but keeping the motorhome on the road and out of the ditches took precedence.

She sighed again and said, "It can wait till later."

There was something in the way she said it that made me not want to wait. It was important to her that I take the time to look at what she'd bought. I figured if it was that important, I'd find a way to do it.

I looked out the side mirror and saw at least ten cars stacked up behind us. There was no way they could safely get around, but sooner or later someone would try. They'd do it going up a hill or around a blind curve, betting their life and those around them they could make it.

It was a bet I didn't want to be a part of.

Seeing a turn-off at a church parking lot about a quarter mile ahead, I flipped on my right turn signal and let the motorhome slow. When we reached the turn, I pulled into the lot and parked.

Abigail looked at me and asked, "Why are we stopping?"

I pointed out the window. "See all those cars going by? They were behind us and I didn't want to hold them up any longer. Plus, I wanted to see what you got me."

Her eyes brightened. But instead of handing me the package, she held it close to her chest and said, "It's really nothing. You probably won't like it. I shouldn't have gotten it."

I smiled. "Abigail, whatever it is, I'm sure I'll like it. Let me see."

She nodded and said, "Okay, I'll give it to you, but you have to promise me something."

I laughed. "Promise you something? Am I going to regret it?"

She shook her head. "No, you won't regret it."

"Okay then. I promise."

She took a deep breath. "You know this morning when Devin introduced us?"

I nodded.

"Well, she introduced me as Abigail. And while that's my real name, I'd like it if you'd call me Abby. But if you don't want to, that's okay."

I smiled. "Abby it is. Now let me see what you bought me."

She held onto the package. "Call me Abby when we're alone. But out in public, call me Paige. Paige Mendoza. And I'll remember to call you Tony. Think you can do that?"

I nodded. "Yeah, you'll be Paige, I'll be Tony. But why? Why can't we use our real names?"

She was quick with an answer. "Look at the credit card. The one Devin gave you. Whose name do you see on it?"

I pulled out the card and saw that it had been issued to Tony Mendoza.

"So I'm supposed to be Tony Mendoza?"

She nodded.

"Okay, I'll be Tony. But what if I have to show another ID? A driver's license?"

Again, she was quick with an answer. She reached into the small shoulder bag she'd been carrying, pulled out a driver's license and handed it to me.

I took the license and looked at it. It had Tony Mendoza's name, a Key West address, my date of birth and my picture.

A recent one.

"Where you'd get this? How'd you get my picture?"

She grinned. "The picture was easy. Found it online. A woman friend of yours posted several on her Facebook page. Be happy I chose that one and not a more embarrassing one."

I knew the photos she was referring to. Taken when I was not at my best. I'd have to talk with the woman who posted them online. She shouldn't have done so without asking me. Maybe she knew I would have said 'no'. Maybe that's why she didn't ask. Still, she needed to take them down.

I looked at the fake driver's license; it looked real. It would fool most people.

"Who made this?"

Abby wagged her finger. "It would be better if you didn't know. Just put it in your wallet. You probably won't need it. But if you do, it's good to know you have it."

Before I could ask another question, she held out the package and said, "Don't you want to see what I got you?"

I did. I took the package and opened it.

Inside there were three CDs—a double CD of *Blue Collar Comedy;* a *John Pinette - Show me the Buffet* CD; and a *Ralphie May - Prime Cut* CD.

I looked up and saw her watching me. She was trying to figure out if I liked her gift or not. Not wanting to keep her in suspense, I smiled and said, "I love them. They'll keep us from getting bored while I drive."

She nodded and said, "That's what I was thinking. Plus, we could listen to them all the way to Vicksburg. Won't that be fun?"

I wasn't sure whether it would be fun or not. The *Blue*

Collar Comedy CD would be clean and a have a lot of laughs. But the other two had Parental Advisory stickers on the cases. I wondered how Abby would handle it when she heard the uncensored truck stop language these comedians used.

I figured I'd probably find out before we reached Vicksburg. But to play it safe, I opened the *Blue Collar* CD and put the first disc in the player. While it was spinning up, I put the motorhome in gear, and when traffic cleared, I pulled back out on the highway and headed north.

Two hours of family friendly laughs later, we had cleared Hattiesburg and were on US 49 heading toward Jackson. Listening to the CDs had made the time pass quickly, and Abby had laughed out loud more than a few times.

When the second disc ended, I pulled it out of the player and asked her to put it back in the case since I couldn't do it while driving. After she put the CD away, she said she was going back to get a bottle of water and wanted to know if I wanted one.

I did.

Bob had come up front when we put the first CD in, but he wasn't real happy when we started laughing. It seemed to scare him, and he headed to the back. Like most cats, he sleeps fifteen to eighteen hours a day, and I didn't expect that to change just because we had a guest on board.

After taking a sip of the water Abby had brought me, I nodded at the unopened CD cases and asked, "You ready to listen to another or do you want to talk for a while?"

We were two hours out from Vicksburg, and I wasn't sure which would be better; talking to her for two hours or listening to a parental advisory comic telling raunchy jokes.

For Abby, it was an easy decision.

Chapter Ten

The unlistened to CDs remained in their unopened cases because Abby wanted to talk.

I started the conversation with a question. "How do you know Kat?"

Before she could answer, her phone started playing the Darth Vader theme announcing an incoming call.

I could only hear one side of the conversation and it went something like this:

"No, I haven't heard from her. I keep trying her phone, but no luck yet."

"We'll be there tomorrow. Tonight we're staying at the casino in Vicksburg. The same one she stayed at."

"We haven't talked about that yet. But we will. It'll work out."

"We're getting along fine. He's been a perfect gentleman."

She laughed and said, "No, I don't think I'll tell him that. Don't want to scare him off."

"I'll call if I hear from her."

"Yeah, I hope you're right."

She ended the call, put the phone in her pocket and looked at me with a curious smile. She didn't say anything; she just stared at me and smiled like someone who knew a secret and wasn't going to share.

We were getting into the outskirts of Jackson and the traffic was starting to build. I had to keep my eyes on the road, but each time I glanced over, she was looking at me, a goofy grin on her face.

I finally said, "What?"

Instead of answering my question, she said, "That was Boris, calling to see if we'd heard from Kat. He wanted to know where we were spending the night and if you were being nice to me.

"You probably heard what I told him."

"Yeah, I heard most of it. But I missed the part where you said, 'I don't think I'll tell him that. It might scare him.'

"What was that about?"

She laughed. "Nothing really, just Boris teasing me about something."

I waited for her to tell me more because I wanted to know what that "something" was, especially if it was something that might scare me off. But Abby didn't elaborate. Instead, she turned and looked at the road ahead. Traffic was starting to back up, and it looked like we weren't going to be moving very fast until we got back out on the interstate.

According to the GPS, it looked like we had to travel about six miles further on US 49 before we would get on I-20 going west. Looking at the long line of cars in front of us and the string of stop lights at every intersection, it was going to take a while.

Abby apparently wasn't bothered by this likely delay. In fact, she looked happy as she sat in the passenger seat, humming softly.

With her being in a good mood, I figured it was a good

time to ask the question I'd asked earlier but hadn't got an answer to.

"So, how do you know Kat?"

Without turning to look at me she said, "We're cousins. Her mother and my mother are sisters."

"So she's family? That's good to know. Do you two hang out much?"

She sighed. "We did when we were kids. We pretty much grew up together. But as we got older, we went our separate ways. She got involved in the family business, and I didn't."

With Boris leading it, I had a pretty good idea what the family business involved and knew better than to ask questions about it. Still, I wanted to know more about Abby's and Kat's relationship.

"When was the last time you spoke with her?"

Abby didn't answer.

Thinking maybe she hadn't heard my question, I repeated it. "Abby, when was the last time you spoke with Kat?"

She shrugged. "I can't remember. It's been a few months."

The strain in her voice when she answered told me she didn't want to talk about it. I didn't see a reason to push it any further, so I didn't.

Instead, I said, "Maybe we should listen to another CD."

Without asking me which one, she put John Pinette in and pressed "Play."

We were soon listening to him tell funny stories about his adventures at a Chinese buffet. He made it sound like a disaster, and we couldn't help but laugh.

An hour later, just as the CD was ending, we saw the first of the Vicksburg exit signs. We had left Jackson behind, gotten on I-20 going west and watched the miles tick off as we got closer to our destination.

Seeing the Vicksburg exit, Abby pulled out her map and looked at the route she had put together. She pointed ahead and said, "Take exit 1A. Then stay right, go up the hill past the casino and you'll see the sign for the RV park.

"Our reservations are for the Mendozas. Tony and Paige. If anyone asks or if you have to sign anything, be sure to use the Mendoza name. It's important."

I was too tired to ask why, but if she wanted me to pretend to be Tony Mendoza, that's who I would be.

Ten minutes later, we were parked in site twenty-seven at the Ameristar Casino RV Park. The people in the office had no problem finding our reservation, and I had no problem signing in as Tony Mendoza.

Like all sites in the Ameristar park, ours was a pull through, which meant I didn't have to worry about backing the RV in. I just turned into the site, pulled up a bit and parked. After killing the motor, I went outside and hooked us up to shore power.

Back inside, I closed all the curtains, giving us privacy, and pushed the button to run the slide room out. The driver's side wall, from just behind the driver's seat to the end of the couch, moved out about thirty inches, almost doubling the amount of floor space inside.

With the slide out and the curtains closed, it was like being back home—everything looked the same. Except Bob and I had company. Abigail.

She had moved back to the couch, and Bob had come up front to join her. He seemed happy we were stopped for the night and I was too. Fifteen hours on the road, driving the big motorhome was about all I could do in a day.

The sun had set about an hour earlier, and by the time we'd gotten to Vicksburg, it was full-on dark. Fortunately, the road to the campground and all the sites in it were well lit. It was easy to see where everything was and I didn't have to worry about hitting anything when we drove in.

We hadn't eaten much since our quick lunch at the Flying J truck stop, eight hours earlier, so I asked Abby if she was hungry. "You ready to eat? I've got TV dinners in the freezer."

She shook her head. "No thanks. No TV dinners tonight. Not when there's a buffet at the casino. Give me a minute to change, we'll go there to eat."

She got up from the couch and headed back to my bedroom. I wasn't sure what she was going to change into, but I was sure it was going to be nicer than what I had on— faded cargo shorts and a light green fishing shirt.

Five minutes later, she returned, and all I could say was, "Wow!"

She was wearing a thigh-length, sleeveless, black cocktail dress with matching black high heels and carrying a small, black purse. Her hair was combed out so that it flowed over her bare shoulders and to me, she looked like a goddess. The transformation was stunning.

She smiled and asked, "You like?"

I nodded. "Yeah, a lot."

She was still smiling when she said, "Good. As soon as you change, we can go. I've laid some clothes out for you."

Had I not been so stunned by her transformation, I might not have been happy about her going through my closet and picking out what I was supposed to wear. But after seeing how great she looked, I'd wear anything she wanted me to, as long as it meant she would be accompanying me for the evening.

Back in my bedroom, I saw she had set out a pair of jeans, a white button up shirt and a belt for me to wear. I quickly put them on, combed my hair and rejoined her up front.

She smiled when she saw me and said, "You look nice."

Then she said, "This is important. We're supposed to be the Mendozas. Once we get inside, don't call me Abby or Abigail. Just Paige. And I'll call you Tony. Got it?"

I nodded. "Yes, Paige, whatever you say."

She smiled and motioned to the door. "The casino shuttle is waiting for us outside. Let's go."

Like a gentleman, I opened the door and helped her out. Then, after making sure I had my wallet, I locked the motorhome and helped Abby, aka Paige, into the shuttle.

Her transformation had changed the dynamic between us. She was no longer the goat girl who had weirdly asked me to wear a wedding ring and had bought me gifts at a truck stop.

She was now something else; but I wasn't quite sure what.

It was a short ride from the RV park to the casino. From the outside, the place looked like an old-time Mississippi river boat. White with a multistory red paddle wheel emblazoned with the word "Ameristar" in neon. Four simulated smoke stacks towering above the top deck added to the illusion.

Even though much of the facade was fake, it was a real boat docked on the Mississippi River. It couldn't ever leave the dock under its own power, but it was a real boat. Mississippi law required it. Casinos in the state had to be on the water like riverboats of the past.

When the shuttle dropped us off at the front door, Abby

grabbed my hand and led me inside. We walked past the rows and rows of slot machines, past the poker room and headed for the escalator leading to the buffet.

There was a short line, and it didn't take long to reach the pay station and get seated. Our server took our drink orders and told us how the buffet worked. We could get anything we wanted and go back as many times as we liked. The only rule was we had to get a new plate each time we returned to the food line.

After the server left, I followed Abby and stayed close to her as we loaded up our plates with food. It wasn't that she needed or even asked me to stay close, I just felt like I wanted to.

We both got the same thing, brazed salmon, wild rice, and steamed broccoli. Probably the healthiest food you could find at a casino buffet.

After finishing off our first plate, we picked up clean plates and went through the dessert line. They had a lot of tempting choices including chocolate cakes, chocolate mousse, chocolate puddings, chocolate pie, chocolate chip cookies, and even a chocolate fountain.

Abby passed on all the chocolate and said key lime pie would go better with the salmon we'd eaten, so we both got a slice and headed back to our seats. The pie turned out to be pretty good. Not as good as what you can get in Key West, but still, better than average for a casino buffet.

After finishing our pie, Abby looked at me and asked, "Have you got the cash Devin gave you from Boris?"

I shook my head. "No, I left it in the motorhome. Why?"

She smiled, "I wanted to borrow a hundred dollars. But if you don't have it, it's okay."

I wasn't sure why she'd need a hundred dollars, but I had

more than that on me and couldn't see any reason not to share it with her.

I pulled out my wallet and picked out a ten and hundred. I put the ten on the table for the server, and instead of giving the hundred to Abby, I kept it hidden in my hand.

I didn't think it would look right, me handing her a hundred-dollar bill in the crowded restaurant. People might get the wrong idea, so I said, "Paige dearest, are you ready to go?"

She nodded, stood and took my hand. When she did, she felt the hundred and smiled. She leaned into me and whispered, "I'll pay you back."

Then she gave me a kiss on the cheek.

Still holding my hand, she led me down the escalator to the nearest cashier cage. She slid the hundred under the bars and got five twenty-dollar chips in return.

With chips in hand, she headed over to the gaming area. She stopped near the slot machines and picked up a white plastic chip bucket and handed it to me. She said, "Hang onto this. We'll need it."

Then she headed to the nearest roulette table. Remembering what Devin had told me about not letting her gamble, I was starting to worry. Maybe she did have a gambling problem. And maybe she was about to lose a lot of my money. I'd soon find out.

There were only two other people at the roulette table, and the dealer was waiting for bets to be placed.

Abby stared at the motionless wheel for a moment then placed all her chips on the square for twenty-eight black. The dealer looked up, apparently surprised that a new player was going all in on one number. According to the small placard, the odds of winning on a single number in roulette were thirty-five to one. After waiting for the two other players to place bets, the dealer announced, "No more bets," and spun the wheel.

When it reached maximum velocity, he dropped a small white ball onto the spinning wheel and we waited to see where it would land.

Chapter Eleven

The two other gamblers at the table were yelling, "Come on, red; come on, red." They were urging the little white ball to settle into any of the red slots. If it did, they would be winners.

Abby didn't say anything; she just watched with a slight smile on her face. She didn't seem worried that she'd just bet the full hundred she'd borrowed on a thirty-five-to-one long shot.

We watched as the little ball hit the first gate and was knocked violently back up against the outside rail. Losing momentum, it fell back onto the spinning wheel and bounced in and out of the numbered slots. With each bounce, it slowed a bit and would soon find a home in either a red or black.

Abby watched intently, saying nothing as the ball made its way around the wheel. She was standing on my left and had taken my hand in hers as soon as the dealer dropped the ball. Her grip had gotten tighter as the ball slowed toward its final destination.

The shouts from the other two betters had taken on a sense of urgency. "Come on, red; come on, red."

The ball slowed, and they cheered as it fell into twenty-one red. But instead of stopping there, the ball bounced out, and when it finally settled, their cheers were replaced with groans.

The dealer called out, "Twenty-eight black. We have a winner."

He quickly retrieved the losing chips and placed them in a hidden slot near his station. Then he counted out thirty-five one-hundred-dollar chips, and slid them over to Abby.

She smiled, picked them up and dropped all but one into the bucket I was holding. The dealer again called out, "Place your bets."

Abby looked at me and shook her head. She whispered, "Let's look for another table."

She turned and scanned the room. After a moment she nodded toward a roulette wheel in the far corner and said, "Over there. That one."

Still holding my hand, she made her way over to the table she'd picked out. The dealer had just spun the wheel, and three people who had placed bets were watching to see if they had won or not.

Abby watched as well. She didn't take her eyes off the wheel until the ball settled. When it did, she whispered, "Not this one."

She turned and scanned the room. After a moment she said, "Over there."

Still holding my hand, she led me to another roulette table. The wheel at that one had been spun and the ball dropped. Abby watched as it circled around until it settled into a red slot. Even though she hadn't bet, she seemed satisfied with the result.

After the winners were paid, the dealer called out, "Place your bets." Abby didn't hesitate; she put one of her hundred-dollar chips on twenty-four black.

The dealer waited for other bets, and, after a minute,

called out, "No more bets." He spun the wheel, and after it got up to speed, he shot the ball against the outside rim. It ran clockwise against the counter clockwise spin of the wheel.

We watched as the ball raced around and listened to bettors near us urging it to drop onto their chosen color. Abby was silent, squeezing my hand as the ball slowed and began the search for its final destination.

When it stopped, there were cheers from the winners and groans from the losers. The dealer called out, "Twenty-four black. We have a winner."

He scooped up the losing bets, paid off the winners and slid another thirty-five one-hundred-dollar chips over to Abby. She picked them up and dropped them into the white tub I was holding. With seventy chips in it, it was starting to get heavy.

In less than twenty minutes, she had won seven thousand dollars by placing two long shot bets on roulette. She was on a hot streak, and I expected her to want to play more. But I was wrong.

She tugged my arm and whispered, "We need to leave." There was urgency in her voice so I didn't argue. She led me over to the nearest money cage and cashed out. I watched as the lady behind the bars count out seven thousand dollars in one-hundred-dollar bills.

She placed them in a white envelope and slid it over to Abby, who picked up the envelope and handed it to me. Then she whispered, "We need to leave, now."

She took my free hand and headed for the casino's front door. We were just a few steps away when a well-dressed woman holding a clipboard stepped in front of us. Abby tried to walk around her, but the woman moved to block us.

Two men wearing suits walked up behind the woman and stood to her side.

She introduced herself as Jen Wilson, head of guest services for the casino. In a very polite voice, she said, "I hope you are enjoying your visit here. As one of our preferred guests, we'd love for you to stay awhile and enjoy all that we have to offer.

"Are you staying here in one of our rooms?"

I shook my head. "No, we're in the RV park."

Abby squeezed my hand. Apparently, she didn't want me telling the woman where we were staying.

Jen Wilson smiled and said, "That's great. But we can do better than that. We can give you two nights in one of our winner's suites overlooking the Mississippi River. On the house, of course. This would include complimentary meals and tickets to tomorrow night's shows. Just say yes, and I'll arrange it for you."

She was all smiles. Friendly as could be. But Abby wasn't having any of it. She said, "We appreciate the offer, but we're leaving early in the morning and have already spent more time here than we planned."

After giving her answer, she made a move to get around the woman, but as before she was blocked. The woman said, "Please reconsider. We don't want you to miss out on staying in one of our premier suites. It has a fantastic view, and we can offer free room service—anything you want from our menu."

Jen Wilson was determined to have us stay. She didn't want us leaving any time soon, especially with Abby's seven-thousand-dollars in roulette winnings.

Abby looked at me, smiled and said, "It would be nice to spend the night in a suite. Maybe we could do it on the way back."

She turned to the woman and said, "We can't do it tonight, but if the offer is good for next week, we'd be happy to take you up on it. Can you give us a voucher we could use when we come back?"

Chapter Twelve

It had been a brilliant move on Abby's part. The casino host had to decide whether it was worth losing a whale by not extending the free room offer to a future date. If she said, "No," chances were good Abby and I would not return to the casino.

But if she did extend the offer, there was a chance we would come back, and the casino might get back some or all of the money that Abby had won.

Instead of answering right away, she tapped her left ear and looked up at an overhead security camera. Apparently, she wanted guidance from above.

After a moment she said, "Yes, we can extend the offer. It'll take a few minutes to get the details printed up. If you'd like to wait over by the bar, we'll bring them to you when they're ready."

Abby smiled. "That's great. But no need to hurry. Just leave it at the guest services desk. We'll pick it up before we leave in the morning."

The woman nodded. "Are you sure you don't want to wait? It'll only take a few minutes. I just need your names and contact info."

Abby squeezed my hand, harder than before. She didn't want me answering the question because she was probably afraid I'd forget about us being the Mendozas.

Jen Wilson was waiting, pen at the ready when Abby

said, "We're the Mendozas. Paige and Tony. From Duck Key, Florida. We'll drop by the guest services desk to pick everything up before we leave in the morning."

While she was writing our names, Abby maneuvered me around the woman, and we headed out the door where the casino shuttle was waiting.

We hopped in and Abby told the driver, "RV park, please."

The driver, not noticing the casino host with clipboard in hand, coming out behind us, put the van in gear and took off.

When we got to the park, the driver asked, "Where can I drop you?"

Abby said, "Site seventeen, please."

I started to tell her it was the wrong site, but she squeezed my hand again. She wanted the driver to think we were in seventeen.

It didn't take him long to find the site. A fifth wheel trailer, hooked to a dually pickup, was parked in it. The driver said, "That's a nice looking rig you got there. Thinking about getting something like it when I retire."

I tipped him a fiver and said, "We sure like it. It's a great way to travel."

He said, "Thanks," and drove away. As soon as he was out of sight, we walked over to number twenty-seven, where our motorhome was parked.

It was exactly as we had left it. No sign that anyone had tried to break in. No note on the windshield telling us to check with the office or a warning that our real names had been discovered and we were being kicked out. There was none of that. Everything looked normal.

I unlocked the door and helped Abby up the steps. I followed her in and was reaching for the light switch when she stood on her tiptoes and kissed me on the lips. Then, without saying anything, she turned and walked to the back bedroom.

I switched on the lights and saw that Bob was coming up front to see what was going on. Normally I would have asked him how his day had been, but I was too stunned by the kiss to say anything. My not asking didn't seem to bother him. He did his normal thing, came up and rubbed against my ankle and then took a seat on the couch.

A few moments later, Abby came up front to join us. She had changed into a loose fitting white T-shirt over white cotton shorts with happy little pink rabbits on them. She moved to the couch, sat down beside Bob and asked, "You have anything to drink in here?"

I did, a box of Chardonnay in the fridge. I didn't tell her about it, at least not right away because Devin had warned me not to let her drink.

But Devin had lied about a lot of things. Maybe even about Abby having a drinking problem.

Abby wasn't a child. Not by any measure. She was close to my own age and hadn't given me any reason to treat her as a child, so I said, "I've got some Chardonnay in the fridge. Would you like some?"

She nodded. I got the wine out and filled her glass. When I handed it to her, she asked, "Aren't you going to join me?"

I shook my head. "No. I have to drive in the morning. I don't want to do it with a hangover."

She looked disappointed with my answer, but it didn't stop her from taking a sip of her wine. She smiled and said, "Maybe you should change into something more comfortable."

I was still wearing jeans and the button up shirt she'd picked out for me. Not really the kind of thing I could relax in, especially since she had changed into something so casual. I pointed to the back and said, "I think I will change. And then you can tell me what happened back there in the casino."

She winked at me as I walked past her on my way to the bedroom. I didn't know what she had in mind, but I needed to stay sober. I didn't need things to get weird between us.

Closing the door behind me, I pulled off my jeans and shirt and put on cargo shorts and a clean T-shirt. When I hung my jeans up in the closet, the envelope with Abby's winnings fell to the floor. I picked it up and put it in my pocket.

Back up front, I saw she had nearly finished off her wine, but I didn't offer to refill her glass. Instead, I tossed the envelope full of cash onto the couch beside her and asked, "How'd you do it?"

She looked up from Bob, who was still in her lap. "What do you mean?"

"The roulette wheel. You picked the winning numbers twice in a row. How'd you do it?"

She shrugged. "Just lucky, I guess."

I wasn't buying it. No one is that lucky. "There's more to it than luck. Tell me how you did it."

She rubbed her eyes with the hand she had been petting Bob with then held her wine glass out to me and said, "Refill it and maybe I'll tell you."

Instead of taking the glass, I crossed my arms and said, "No. First, tell me how you did it, and then I'll pour you another."

Her lips formed a pout as she thought about her answer. Then she said, "If I tell you, you'll think I'm weird. I don't want you to think that."

I laughed. "Abby, it's too late. I already think you're weird. But in a good way."

She saw me smile and nodded. "Okay, I'll tell you, but you're not going to believe me."

She continued, "Sometimes I can see the future. Not too far in the future and not like someone reading a crystal ball. It's just that if I look at something, I can sometimes see what's going to happen next.

"That's the way it worked with the roulette wheel. On the first one, the number twenty-eight popped up in my head. So I bet on it. And it won.

"When we moved to the second wheel, I got a blank. I don't know why, but it was like it was saying, "Don't bet on me."

"When we moved over to the third wheel, I saw the number twenty-four right away and knew it would win. I bet on it, and it did.

"That's all I can tell you. Sometimes I see things."

I nodded. Had I not seen it with my own eyes, I wouldn't have believed her, but after seeing her pick two winning numbers in a row, it was hard not to.

"What about lottery numbers? Do you ever see the winning numbers before they're drawn?"

She shook her head. "No, it doesn't work that way. I have to be physically close or have some personal connection for it to work. The lottery is too remote, too random."

What she said kind of made sense. But I had another

question. "Since the roulette wheels were speaking to you, why didn't you stay and win more?"

She held out her empty glass. "No more answers until you refill me."

Chapter Thirteen

I'd been warned not to let Abby get drunk. But it was just wine, and I'd only poured her half a glass. I couldn't see how a bit more would hurt. I refilled her glass, being sure to stop about halfway.

She took a sip, put the glass down and said, "The casino people, they always want to talk to you if you start winning too much. I learned that the hard way.

"So what you have to do is win quickly and then leave. Don't make a scene; don't attract a crowd. Just win and leave. That's what I was trying to do back there. Get out before we were noticed.

"And we almost made it. If it hadn't been for the clipboard lady, we would have. The security people watching the cameras must have alerted her. They do that with the big winners; they watch them as they move through the casino.

"When it looks like a winner is getting ready to leave, they have a hostess step in. They'll thank the winner and give them a reason to stay longer or to come back.

"Some places are worse than others. This one wasn't bad. The lady was nice and didn't make us stay any longer than we wanted to. She even offered us a free suite."

I nodded. "So you told them we were the Mendozas. If you didn't want them to know who we were, why not make up another name? Something different?"

Abby picked up her glass and took a sip before she

answered. "It's your fault. You told them we were staying in the RV park. If I gave them a different name, they could look it up in the RV reservation system and know it was fake. That would look suspicious, a big winner using a fake name. So I gave them the same name we used when we checked in, the Mendozas.

I nodded. She was pretty good at this. Like maybe it was how she made a living. I asked her about it. "So, you've dealt with casinos before?"

She took another sip. "Yeah, a few times. Nothing regular. Just when I need to make some quick cash."

"You always win?"

She shook her head. "No, not always. It looks too suspicious if you always win. Sometimes I lose or I keep my bets small so as not to draw attention.

"Like I said, I don't do it very often. But when I do, I go in, win a couple of times and leave."

She had finished her wine and set it on the table beside the couch. Bob jumped off her lap and ran to the back bedroom. Being free of his weight, she picked up the envelope with her casino winnings and pulled out five one-hundred-dollar bills. She held them out to me. "Here's the hundred I owe you, plus interest."

I didn't need the money. She probably knew that. She probably also knew I wouldn't take what she was offering. If she could see the future, she knew that before she pulled the money out.

I shook my head. "You keep it. Maybe we'll need it later."

She didn't argue. She put the money back in the envelope and asked, "This couch fold out into a bed?"

"Yeah, it does. You ready to sleep?"

She yawned and said. "I am. You mind setting it up while I go back and get ready?"

I smiled. "No, not at all. It'll be ready when you get back up here."

She nodded and went to the back.

I was happy it looked like there would be no bedtime drama about who was sleeping where. I opened the overhead compartment, got the sheets and pillows out and set the couch up as a bed. I made sure everything looked comfy so when she came back up front she wouldn't complain about sleeping on the jackknife sofa.

She spent a bit of time in the bathroom, washing her face and doing whatever else women do before they go to bed. When she came out, she said, "I'll see you in the morning." And then, instead of coming up front and getting on the couch, she stepped into *my* bedroom and locked the door behind her.

I wasn't sure what she was thinking. It was understood she was to sleep on the couch and I was going to sleep in my own bed. That's the way it worked in my motorhome, guests on the couch and me on my bed.

I needed to explain it to her.

I went back and tapped on the bedroom door. "Abby, I probably should have mentioned this earlier. You're on the couch tonight. Not me."

From the other side of the door, she said, "That's not the way I see it. I'm the guest, so I get the bed. You get the couch."

I tapped on the door again. "Abby, don't make this difficult. That's my bed in there. That's where I sleep. You're supposed to be on the couch."

I waited for her reply, but there was nothing but silence.

I tried again. "Abby, the couch. That's where you're supposed to sleep."

This time, she replied. "Walker, I've seen the future. It shows me sleeping in this bed tonight and you on the couch. I can't change it. That's the way the future works."

I shook my head. She was using her so-called gift to tell me why I was wrong about where I'd be sleeping. It wasn't a fair fight. If she could see the future, she already knew the outcome. Even if she couldn't see the future, there wasn't much I could do to change the situation. She had locked the door and I wasn't getting in.

It was clear I wasn't going to win this one. She'd claimed the bed, and she wasn't going to give it up. My only option was to sleep on the couch. So instead of fuming about it, I took care of my bathroom duties, went back up front, and settled in for the night.

A couple of hours later, I woke to the sounds of Bob scratching on the bedroom door. He was on the outside, wanting in. I knew from past experience he wouldn't quit until the door was opened. He didn't care who was on the bed. He didn't care if she could see the future or not. All he knew was the bed is where he slept at night, and he wanted in.

He worked on the door for five minutes, scratching and crying, making sure that whoever was in there knew he wasn't going to go away.

Eventually, Abby gave in and opened the door for him. As soon as she did, I heard him huff his displeasure about being locked out, followed by his footsteps as he ran for the bed. He was soon in his favorite spot, between the pillow and the window. Abby would have to make room for him, whether she liked it or not.

This time, she didn't bother to close or lock the door. Maybe she knew that if she did, she'd have to get up and let Bob back out later on. He liked to use his litter box in the middle of the night and would make sure he got his way.

I drifted off to sleep, wondering how much of the future Abby could really see.

The next morning, when I woke, she was gone. The door to the bedroom was open and the bed nicely made. The bathroom door was open, and the room had been cleaned up as well. But Abby was nowhere to be found. She wasn't in the back or up front. It was clear that she was gone.

I pulled on my shoes and went to the side door to check outside. The door was unlocked which meant she had gone out that way, and not locked it behind her. I grabbed my keys and headed out to look for her.

Out in the parking lot I could see several of the other campers getting ready for the road. They were unhooking from shore power, cranking down their TV antennas, and raising their leveling jacks.

They were doing what I should have been doing. Instead, I was standing in the parking lot, looking for the woman who had slept in my bed the night before.

Chapter Fourteen

She showed up ten minutes later wearing a white V-neck T-shirt tucked into cut-off jean shorts. Black Doc Martens on her feet, mirrored sunglasses hiding her eyes, and a large plastic bag slung over her shoulder.

When she saw me, she said, "Glad to see you finally got up. Hope you're hungry because I brought breakfast."

I nodded. "You went back to the casino?"

She smiled. "Yeah, I did. I woke up early. Didn't want to disturb you and didn't have anything else to do, so I went back up there."

I pointed at a white envelope sticking out of the bag she was carrying. "What's that?"

"Everything we need to get the free suite when we come back. Plus coupons for free meals and shows."

She was proud of what she had gotten. But I had a question.

"I thought you said they'd want to see my driver's license before they'd give you that stuff."

She smiled. "They did. That's why I took your wallet with me. I showed them your Mendoza license, and that's all they needed."

"Wait, you took my wallet?"

"I had to. It was the only way I could get the freebies. Plus I needed some small bills to pay for breakfast. Hope you don't mind."

I did mind. She'd left without telling me where she was going. She took my wallet and showed my fake driver's license to casino security. I wasn't happy with any of it. But I had to be careful with what I said and how I said it. I didn't want to start the day out wrong by setting her off. So I calmly said, "You slept in my bed last night. You took my wallet this morning. You showed my driver's license to hotel security. And you used my money to buy breakfast? Am I missing anything?"

She smiled. "No, that's pretty much it. You hungry?"

I was. And even though she had done just about everything she could to make me mad, she'd come back with food. That was her saving grace. I couldn't stay mad if I wanted to eat.

She'd bought the Grand Slam breakfast at one of the casino's cafes, one for her and one for me, eggs, sausage, grits and biscuits. No coffee, but that was okay. I had juice in the fridge.

We set the food on the dinette and proceeded to chow down. Between bites, I asked a few questions.

"They recognize you when you went in?"

She shook her head. "No, new people on duty."

"You go back to the roulette wheel?"

"Yeah."

"You win?"

She tossed me my wallet. "Look inside."

I wasn't worried about her taking money out of my wallet. Not for breakfast or anything else. I didn't feel the need to check, so I didn't. I pushed the wallet away.

But she persisted. "Go ahead, check it. I want you to."

I'd been down this road with her before. She didn't give up when she wanted to get her way and probably wouldn't give up this time either. I shrugged and opened the wallet.

In addition to the three hundred dollars that had been there the night before, there was now another three hundred.

I looked up at her. "You get lucky again?"

She nodded.

"At roulette?"

She nodded again.

"They stop you on the way out?"

"Not this time. I only bet ten dollars. Won once and left."

I smiled. "Good."

When we finished eating, I asked, "You ready to get back on the road?"

"Yeah, but I need to try Kat's phone again."

She punched in her number and listened as the call connected. As before, it went directly to voice mail. Kat wasn't answering.

Abby put her phone down and cleaned off the table. She put the empty food containers in a plastic bag and said, "I'll take these out and put them in the trash while you get everything else ready."

While she was outside, I went to the back and topped off Bob's food and water bowls. The smell from his litter box was starting to grow. One more day and it'd be time to clean it out. It wasn't a job I was looking forward to, but it was one of the responsibilities of living with a cat.

When Abby came back in, she asked, "We ready?"

I pointed to the door. "Almost. I need to go out and unhook from shore power. If you need to do anything in the bathroom, now's the time."

I stepped outside and went around to the power pedestal and unhooked us. I rolled up the power cord and stowed it in the utility compartment. Then I did a quick walk around and checked the tires. I made sure we weren't leaving anything behind. People with motorhomes do that often— leave chairs, grills, other things they forget.

I'd once left a woman behind.

She had stepped out at a service station when I was on the other side pumping gas. I didn't see her get out and thought she was still inside when I pulled away. A few miles down the road she called and let me know that I'd left her. She was pretty upset. Being left behind at a gas station in the heat of the summer in the Everglades is never a pleasant experience.

It had been my mistake. One that I vowed to never make again. And, yes, I went back and got her.

After doing the walk-around outside, I went back inside. Abby had raised the shades and the sun streamed in, letting us know it was time to hit the road. Our destination was three hundred miles north, and we wanted to get there well before dark.

I started the motorhome to let it warm up, but it didn't take the Ford V-10 long. Less than two minutes later, the gauges on the dash showed everything was in good shape. Oil pressure, water temp and amp meter right where they should be. No check engine lights, no problems. We were good to go.

Leaving our site in the casino campground, we went south on business 61 for a mile and then took the ramp onto

I-20 west. Two hundred yards later, we crossed the Mississippi River into Louisiana.

Unlike the rolling hills of Mississippi, the terrain in that part of Louisiana is flat and bordered on both sides by wide open delta. The land is low, the soil black, and the highway straight.

We were making good time toward our next scheduled stop, the Love's travel plaza at the Tallulah exit. According to Abby, Kat had stopped there for gas on her way north, and we were going to do the same.

It didn't take us long to get there. Just twenty minutes after crossing the Mississippi River, we took exit 171, which led us into to the Love's Travel Stop.

As with most truck stops, the parking lot was easy to get into with wide open spaces and few obstacles. It had been designed to make it easy for tired truck drivers to get there eighteen wheelers in and out of without hitting anything. The wide open lot design worked for RVs as well.

The big trucks had their own fuel islands with super-fast diesel pumps; these were located behind the Love's store. The rest of us filled up in the islands up front. With the size of the RV, I always looked for the easiest fuel lane to get into. Usually, it was the one on the far right.

As luck would have it, there was no one at that pump, so I pulled in and lined the motorhome's fuel door up with the gas pump nozzle. I'd learned to do this, having discovered that gas pump hoses rarely stretched the length of the motorhome.

We had traveled two hundred and fifty miles since last fueling up and the gas gauge was showing we were down to a quarter tank. It was going to take a while to fill.

I turned to Abby. "You getting out?"

She nodded. "Yeah, I'm going inside to look around. You need anything?"

"Yeah. Chocolate chip cookies. And a can of Mountain Dew."

She shook her head in fake disgust and said, "You're weird." Then she got out and walked to the Love's travel store entrance. The building was divided into three sections, an Arby's restaurant on the left, a convenience store in the middle and a small casino on the far right. I watched as she made her way across the parking lot until she was safely inside.

While I waited for her return, I got out and pumped gas. I put the nozzle in the tank, set the handle to automatic and let it fill. The island had a squeegee sitting in what looked to be fairly clean water so I used it to clean the bugs off the windshield. We'd built up quite a collection coming through Alabama, and they needed to be gone.

After cleaning the windshield, I checked the gas pump and saw that it had shut off at twenty-seven gallons. That was about right for the two hundred and fifty miles we'd traveled. The motorhome was getting just under ten miles a gallon which was not bad for a five-ton vehicle with the aerodynamics of a brick.

Another motorhome had pulled up behind me, waiting for their turn at the pump and not wanting to hold them up, I got in and pulled over to the RV parking area. It was on the right side of the lot, facing the casino.

Abby had yet to return, so I used the time to check on Bob. He hadn't been riding up front with us, which meant he was probably back in the bed. I hadn't seen him all morning and wanted to be sure we hadn't left him back in Vicksburg.

It didn't take long for me to find him. He was where I

thought he'd be; in the bed. Lying in the middle, licking his man parts. He looked up at me with an expression that seemed to say, "What, you don't do this?"

I could only laugh. I left him to his business and checked the bathroom. I wanted to make sure the water pump hadn't been left on. If it had, and if somehow the plumbing had sprung a leak, the pump could run continuously, pumping water onto the floor until the holding tank was dry.

It had happened to me once before. After a long drive over a very rough road, the cold-water joint at the shower head had cracked. The water pump was on and for two hours it pumped a steady stream of water into the shower stall. By the time I discovered the problem, the fresh water tank was empty and the water pump had burned out.

But I'd been lucky. The break was in the shower, where the water could drain harmlessly away. If it had been under the sink or behind the toilet, it could have flooded the bathroom floor. And that would have been an expensive repair.

Fortunately, all I needed was a two-dollar plastic joint for the shower head and a sixty-dollar replacement water pump.

From that, I'd learned an important lesson; when traveling over rough roads, turn off the water pump. Or risk a flooded floor.

While in the bathroom, I noticed the smell from the litter box had gotten stronger. If I was traveling alone, I'd let it go another day. But with a guest on board, it was time to clean it.

I kept the litter box hidden behind the curtain in the shower stall. It gave Bob a bit of privacy when he used it and also meant I didn't have to look at his doings every time I went into the bathroom.

I grabbed two of the grocery bags I kept in the bottom drawer of the vanity, doubled them up, and used the yellow litter scoop I'd bought at the dollar store to clean the clumps out of his box. When I was done, I tied off the bags and took them to the front of the motorhome.

My plan was to dump them in one of the many trash bins that lined the Love's parking lot. Looking out the window to find the nearest one, I spotted Abby heading toward the motorhome. She had a large white Styrofoam cup in one hand, a plastic grocery bag hooked over her shoulder, and a brightly-colored floppy hat on her head.

I stepped out of the motorhome and dropped the bag of litter into the nearest waste bin, and went over to see if I could help Abby with the things she was carrying. When I got close, I asked, "You need help with any of that?"

She had her head down, sipping through the red straw coming out of her drink cup and hadn't seen me. Her view had been blocked by the wide brim of her new hat. She was surprised to see me standing in her path, but she got over it quickly. She held her drink out toward me and said, "Try this. You'll like it."

I wasn't sure I'd like anything that came in an unmarked foam cup bought at a casino truck stop. But, against my better judgment, I took a sip.

Chapter Fifteen

The liquid was sweet but burned my throat as it made its way down into my gut. One sip was all I needed. I handed the drink back to Abby.

"What's in it?"

She smiled. "Orange juice, Mountain Dew and Red Bull. A truck driver showed me how to mix it up. He said it was a sure cure for shyness."

That didn't sound right to me. "A truck driver mixed this up for you? Are you sure he didn't put anything else in it when you weren't looking?"

We'd made it back to the motorhome, and I'd helped her inside. With the door closed behind us, I repeated my question. "Are you sure the guy didn't put anything extra in your drink?"

She shook her head. "I'm sure because he didn't touch it. I bought the ingredients myself, and he showed me how to mix them. He didn't touch anything."

She took another sip, smiled and said, "It's pretty good, don't you think?"

I wasn't sure what I thought. All I knew was it had a pretty good kick and burned on the way down.

"How much of it have you had?"

She grinned. "Enough to know I won't be shy anytime soon."

She put the cup down and opened the plastic bag she'd been carrying. Reaching inside, she pulled out a can of Mountain Dew and handed it to me.

"This is for you."

I took the can and was glad to see it was ice cold, the way I like it.

She reached back into the bag and pulled out a flat of what looked like home-made chocolate chip cookies. "These are for you too. But you'll have to share."

Instead of handing me the cookies, she put them on the kitchen counter. She then reached back into the bag and pulled out a camo print floppy hat.

"I got this for you so we'd match. Put it on."

I knew I'd look silly wearing it, but if it made her happy and would get us back on the road any quicker, I was game.

I put the hat on and moved my head side to side so she could see what it looked like. She frowned and said, "You're really not a hat person, are you?"

Based on her response, I guessed I wasn't. I took the hat off, grabbed the Mountain Dew and went up front. I waited for Abby to join me so we could get back on the road. But she was in no hurry. She sat down at the dinette and said, "Bring me the map, please."

I sighed. I just wanted to get back on the road. I didn't need a map. I knew the way. We had to go north to get to Arkansas, and there was only one road from Love's going that direction.

Reluctantly, I grabbed the atlas and joined her at the table. I opened it to the page showing Louisiana and pointed to where we were parked. I could have shown her the road we were going to take, but I didn't. I wanted to see what she had in mind.

She looked at the map closely, moved her finger along the blue line for US highway 65 north and said, "This is the way we're going, right?"

It was a question with an easy answer. "Yep, that's the way. We'll stay on 65 until we get just beyond Pine Bluff, then we take 270 into Hot Springs. If we leave now, we'll be there in four hours."

She seemed satisfied with my answer and said, "Good. Let's hit the road."

I closed the atlas, took it back up front and stowed it in the pocket behind the driver's seat. I started the motorhome and waited for Abby to join me. She had gone back to the bedroom to put something away. Then, after a moment, she came strolling up front, drink in hand, humming a tune that sounded familiar, most likely from a TV commercial.

After she sat and buckled herself in, I eased away from the Love's parking lot and headed back across the interstate and got us on US 65, heading north. Unlike the wide open four to six lanes of the interstate, US 65 was an older, two-lane blacktop going through small, forgotten rural towns of Louisiana.

It was bordered on the east by high dirt levees that kept the Mississippi River at bay, and on the left by flat fields of withering corn stalks and other crops that had been recently harvested.

The speed limit was fifty-five on most stretches of the road but dropped down to thirty-five when going through the small towns that popped up every few miles.

Of these, Transylvania was the most famous, but only because its name had a connection to Dracula. The town itself was just three buildings, the Transylvania Post Office (a popular place for tourists to mail letters), the Transylvania Elementary School (home of the vampires), and the Transylvania Exxon and Tire Center.

I was surprised Abby didn't say anything about the strange name of the town as we drove through. I looked over and saw that she had closed her eyes and might have been dozing. Maybe the high from the truck stop drink had worn off or maybe she was just bored. It was easy to get that way when riding as a passenger in a motorhome. Nothing to do but watch the world go by mile after mile.

Twenty minutes later, just as we were leaving Lake Providence, she woke with a start and said, "Pull over! Now!"

We were doing fifty on a two-lane road, with no shoulders and nowhere to pull over. I lifted off the gas and asked, "What's wrong? Are you sick?"

She pointed ahead. "That gas station up there. Pull in."

The station had been abandoned a long time ago. The sign had been stolen, the windows had been broken out, the pumps long gone. There was nothing left but the sad shell of someone's failed dream.

"You want me to pull in there?"

"Yes, pull in and stop."

The way she said it convinced me she was sick and needed to get out. Maybe the truck stop drink was the problem. Whatever the reason, I slowed and turned onto the crumbling asphalt that had once been the station's driveway. Trying to avoid the broken glass near the abandoned building, I parked on the edge of the lot, close to the road.

I turned to Abby. "Are you okay?"

She nodded. "Yes."

I expected her to tell me more or for her to get up and head back to the bathroom. But she did neither. She just sat in silence.

I finally asked, "Why are we here?"

She looked at me, cocked her head and said, "I don't know. I just had a feeling we needed to stop. There's a connection to Kat here, but I don't know what it is."

I took a deep breath and sighed loudly. Then asked, "We going to be here long? Should I kill the motor?"

She was staring out the passenger window and didn't answer right away. Finally, she turned to me and said, "I don't know how long we're going to be here. Why don't you go back and check on Bob? I'll call you when I'm ready to leave."

I killed the motor, got up and went back to see Bob. If Abby didn't want me up front with her, it was fine by me. We were only a few hours away from our destination and the day was still young. If she wasn't in a hurry, I wasn't either.

I found Bob on the bed and I decided to join him. When I lay down beside him, he said, "Muurrph."

I said, "Yeah Bob, I know. She's weird."

Chapter Sixteen

With the window in the bedroom, I had a good view of the abandoned gas station outside. Like many of the older ones, the building was divided into two parts. On the right, a small glassed-in office. On the left, a roll up garage door where cars could be pulled in and worked on.

More than likely, there would have been a single bathroom behind the building. When the station was open, travelers could get a key from the office and use it to get inside the washroom. If they were lucky, the toilet would be semi-clean and the facility would be useable.

Back in the day, the station was probably a welcome sight. Gas, water, air and bathroom. A mechanic on duty who could try to figure out why the old jalopy was overheating.

All that was long gone. Now it was just an empty building with a sagging roof, busted down doors, and broken windows. Thieves had stripped away everything of value.

As I looked at the forlorn building, I saw movement in what looked like a bundle of rags blown against the southernmost outside wall. I looked closer, thinking maybe it was an animal rooting around for food, maybe a lost dog.

As I focused on the movement, I could see it wasn't a wild animal. It was a woman with a black trash bag over her body, huddled against the wall. I couldn't see her features well enough to be certain, but it could have been Kat.

I went up front to tell Abby. She looked at me and said,

"What?"

I pointed out the window. "Over there, against the wall. Do you see her?"

Abby looked where I pointed, squinted her eyes, and after a moment, said, "Yes!"

She turned to me and said, "Stay here." Then she got out and walked slowly toward the woman.

As she got closer, the woman saw her coming and tried to make herself invisible. But it was too late, Abby had seen her, and she couldn't hide.

When Abby was about ten feet away, she stopped and asked, "Are you okay?"

The woman lifted her head. I could clearly see she wasn't Kat. She looked at Abby warily, then grunted something that sounded like, "I'm fine."

Abby didn't believe her. "Do you need help?"

The woman again looked at her, then at the motorhome, then back at Abby. "Are you going to hurt me?"

Abby held up both hands in a calming motion. "No, we're not going to hurt you. Do you need a ride? Maybe something to eat or drink?"

The woman struggled to stand. She'd been sitting a long time; her joints were stiff. When she finally got to her feet, she pulled the black trash bag over her head and dropped it on the ground beside her. She was wearing jeans, a gray long sleeve sweat-shirt and tennis shoes. Other than her hair being a mess, she looked like a college student coming home from spring break.

She rubbed her neck, looked at Abby, and smiled. "I'm Grace. I'm trying to get home. Lost my ride and had to spend the night here. If you're going north and promise you're not going to hurt me, I'd be grateful for a lift."

Abby went over to stand close to the woman. They talked, saying things I couldn't hear. Then Abby pointed to the motorhome and Grace nodded. She walked back to where she had been sleeping, moved a pile of rags, and retrieved a small suitcase.

With case in hand, she and Abby walked back to the motorhome. Not wanting to spook them, I moved to the driver's seat and sat. I would do nothing until Abby introduced me.

They came in the side door, Abby first followed by Grace. Abby immediately pointed at me and said, "That's Walker. He's one of the good guys. You won't have to worry about him."

Grace smiled and nodded. I nodded back.

Abby pointed to the back of the motorhome. "There's a bathroom back there. If you feel like using it, you can."

Grace set her suitcase on the floor and said, "If you don't mind, I'd like to wash my face and hands."

Abby nodded. "Go ahead. Make yourself at home. When you come back, we'll get you something to eat."

Grace started toward the back, but stopped and asked, "Is there anyone else in here?"

Abby shook her head. "No, it's just me and Walker. And his cat, Bob. No one else."

She seemed relieved. "Good, I'll be right back."

She stepped into the bathroom and closed the door behind her. Since I figured she'd want to use the sink, I turned on the water pump, using the switch on the dash. It started running almost immediately, delivering water to the bathroom fixtures.

A few minutes later, Grace returned. She had washed the road dirt off her face and hands and combed out the tangles in her hair. She looked to be about twenty-five, maybe two inches taller than Abby. Not skinny, but not overweight either. No visible tattoos, no needle marks, no scars. Short but manicured nails. I was still thinking she could have been a college student.

Abby invited her to take a seat at the dinette and asked me to bring the atlas and join them. Before she sat, Abby grabbed three bottles of water from the fridge and the unopened package of chocolate chip cookies she'd bought at Love's.

It looked like we were going to have an impromptu picnic.

Abby handed one of the bottles to Grace, and then opened the cookies. When I sat, she pointed at them and said, "I know you want one."

I did.

After I took a cookie, Abby got one and moved the package closer to Grace so she could get one as well.

With the three of us sitting at the dinette, in the parking lot of an abandoned gas station at the edge of Lake Providence, Louisiana, Abby turned to Grace and asked, "So what's a nice girl like you doing at a place like this?"

Chapter Seventeen

Grace almost choked upon hearing the question. She laughed and said, "Spending the night at abandoned gas station wasn't part of my plan. I had a ride that supposedly was going to take me all the way to the state line. But he started getting frisky, and I made him let me out.

"I tried thumbing another ride, but not many people pick up hitchhikers around here after dark. I couldn't find any places to stay, so when I got to the gas station, I figured it was better than sleeping in a ditch.

"My plan was to get some sleep, then get up early and catch a ride north. But that didn't work out. There were wild animals roaming around. I kept hearing them getting closer and closer and I was afraid to sleep. When the sun finally came up, I guess I dozed off. When I woke, you were standing there."

Abby nodded. "Sounds like you had a rough night. I'm glad we stopped and saw you. You said you were trying to get home. Where's that?"

Her answer caught us by surprise.

"Hot Springs."

When neither Abby nor I said anything, she continued.

"My brother has an auto repair shop there. I work in the office. There's an apartment above the shop; that's where I live."

Abby nodded. "Hot Springs? Really? That's where we're

going, just past it to the crystal mine in Jessieville."

Grace's face lit up with a smile. "That's amazing! You're the first people who stopped for me, and you're going right past where I live. It's like divine intervention. I prayed for something like this and I guess my prayers were heard."

She picked up her water and took a sip. I watched but didn't say anything. She and Abby were connecting and I didn't want to do anything to break the mood.

Grace put her bottle back on the table and looked at Abby, then at me, and shook her head. "I can't believe you stopped and picked me up. It's a miracle. I could have died out there. Something could have happened during the night, and no one would ever have found me. I am so grateful you came along."

Abby smiled and said, "We're happy we found you."

She pointed at the cookies. "If you're hungry for more, I can make a sandwich. Or, if you want, we can stop in Lake Village and get a burger or something."

Grace smiled and said, "I don't want to put you out. Do what you'd do if I weren't here. I'll just sit back and enjoy the ride."

With that said, I started to get up and go back to the driver's seat, but Grace had a question.

"I don't want to be nosy, but why the crystal mine in Jessieville? Are you diggers?"

Abby laughed. "Diggers? Not me. Walker might be one, but I'm not. We're going to the mine looking for a friend of ours. She was camping there last week, and now she's missing. We're trying to find her."

Grace's eyes got wide. "Are we talking about Coleman Crystal mine? In Jessieville? Because I was there last week.

All day Friday. Maybe I saw your friend."

Abby cocked her head. "You were at the crystal mine? Why?"

Grace smiled and moved her hand to the collar of her sweat-shirt. She reached in and pulled out a silver chain. On the end, a clear quartz crystal. She held it out so Abby could see it.

"I make jewelry from crystals. I went there Friday to dig, trying to get my mind off the funeral I had to go to in Baton Rouge.

"That's where I was coming back from. I took the bus down but wanted to save money on the way back, so I hitched with a friend. Turned out not to be the best idea.

"But yeah, I was at the crystal mine in Jessieville Friday. What does your friend look like?"

Abby looked at me for the answer. "You have a picture of her on your phone, don't you?"

I did, but I didn't know how Abby knew. She'd never asked, and I hadn't mentioned it to her.

I'd taken several photos of Kat the week we camped together on Florida's nature coast. Most of them with her clothes on.

I pulled out my phone and scrolled through the photos until I found one of Kat standing in front of her new motorhome. She was smiling and looked happy. It was the last time I saw her.

I showed it to Grace.

She looked at it carefully, moving in close, trying to get a better angle. She started shaking her head. "I don't know. It was crowded there on Friday, what with the Rainbow people and all. I might have seen her, but, if I did, I didn't notice anything about her or who she was with. What was she driving? Maybe she parked close to me in the lot."

Abby answered, "She was in her motorhome, the one in the photo. It was probably parked in the campground."

Grace frowned. "I drove past the campground, but it's up in the trees, and I didn't see any of the campers."

Abby nodded. "That's okay. It was a long shot at best. She may not have even been there Friday. You mentioned the Rainbow people. Who are they?"

Grace shook her head, frowning with disapproval. "They're a bunch of hippies who come in each fall and camp out in the Ouachita National Forest. They show up in school buses and vans and all sorts of broken down cars and trucks. Their camp is just north of Jessieville.

"The newspaper said there were over a thousand them camping out there this year, playing loud music, smoking pot, running around naked and doing who knows what. I've never been out there. Too many weirdos for me.

"There was a bunch of them at the crystal mine when I was there Friday. They're easy to recognize, wearing their tie-dyed T-shirts and hemp beanies, pretending to look for crystals while trying to recruit new members."

Grace was silent for a moment then said, "If you don't find your friend at the mine, you might want to check the Rainbow camp. Maybe she went over there to take a look."

Abby nodded. "We'll definitely do that."

Grace put her hand over her mouth to stifle a yawn, and then looked down at the map I had put on the table earlier. She smiled but didn't say anything.

Since it looked like we were through talking, at least for the moment, I said, "I'm going to get us back on the road. If you girls need anything, let me know."

I went up front and got the motorhome started. I looked back in the mirror to make sure both Abby and Grace were seated. I didn't want to pull out onto the road with either of them standing.

They had both moved to the couch. Bob had come up front and joined them. He had squeezed in between the two women and was soaking up all the attention they were giving him.

With everything secure in the back, I checked traffic and pulled back out on the road and headed north. Hot Springs was four hours away.

Chapter Eighteen

Thirty minutes after getting back on the road, Abby came up front to join me. She settled in on the passenger seat and nodded. She seemed happy.

A few minutes later, she leaned over and whispered, "Grace is sleeping on the couch. She had a rough night and could barely keep her eyes open while we were talking.

"I told her to get some rest. We'll wake her when we get to Hot Springs."

It sounded like a good plan to me. Having filled up with gas at Love's, we had enough gas to get there without having to stop again.

An hour later, we crossed the Arkansas state line and the two-lane road widened to four. It was in good condition and we had no problem cruising at the speed limit. There were a few small towns where the posted limit dropped to thirty-five. A couple of these had stop lights, but most didn't, usually just a cluster of three or four buildings on the side of the road. We'd slow down as required and then get back to cruising speed after passing through.

The only city of size was Pine Bluff and we could smell it long before we got there. They have a big paper mill just outside of town, and the pungent rotten egg smell hits you hard. Had I not known about the mill, I would have thought one of us had gotten really sick from something we ate. The smell was that bad.

But I knew what it was and told Abby about it as soon as I got the first whiff. As it got stronger, we covered our noses with our shirts and tried not to breathe too deeply. I kept wondering how the locals could put up with it.

Somewhere along the line, I'd learned they called it the "smell of money," because the paper mills had created a lot of jobs and boosted the local economy. Still, there wouldn't be enough money to get me to put up with it.

It didn't seem to bother Grace; she slept right through it, or pretended to.

Ten miles north of Pine Bluff, we got off the four-lane and onto US270, the two-lane road that would take us through the piney woods and rolling hills of southern Arkansas all the way to Hot Springs.

Surprisingly, the road was in excellent condition. There was almost no traffic and the motorhome had no problem with the small hills. I set the cruise control to fifty-five and enjoyed the drive.

Fifteen miles outside of Hot Springs, I turned to Abby and said, "It's time to wake her. She needs to show us the way."

I'd been to Hot Springs before and pretty much knew how to get through town, but I didn't know where Grace lived or where she wanted us to drop her off. If it were on the south side of town, we could take the bypass; but if it were on the north, we would have to go through downtown, past the national park and Bath House Row.

I watched in the rear-view mirror as Abby sat down on the edge of the couch and tapped Grace's shoulder. She said, "Grace, we're almost there. Hot Springs."

She had to say it twice, louder the second time, before Grace heard her and woke. She sat up, stretched and looked out the window. We had gotten to Jones Mill, a small town on the outskirts of Hot Springs and Grace immediately knew where she was.

She stretched again and said, "That was quick. How long did I sleep?"

Abby answered, then helped Grace get up off the couch and led her up front. She put her in the passenger seat beside me and then she went back to the couch.

I turned to her and asked, "Where can I take you?"

She smiled. "My brother's shop. It's on the north side of town at the junction of highway 5 and 7. Best way to get there is to stay on 270 until you get to highway 7 and then go north."

I nodded. Highway 7 would take us through the old part of Hot Springs, the downtown area through the national park and past Bath House Row. From there it would go north toward Jessieville and the crystal mine.

Even if Grace hadn't been with us, this was the way we would have gone.

For the most part, after reaching the city limits, it was stop and go traffic. Not too much congestion, just a lot of stop lights as inbound visitors were funneled into the valley where the national park and hot water springs were located.

Sitting up high in the motorhome, we had a grand view of the city as we passed through. Abby had never visited, so Grace told her the history of the places we passed. She explained that even though Hot Springs was famous for the hot water that bubbled out of the ground, all the springs except for one had been capped by the park service. The water was way too hot to get into, and it was deemed too dangerous to leave the springs open to the public.

So instead, the hot water was piped from the capped

springs into the bath houses that lined Central Avenue. For more than a hundred and fifty years, people from all over the world had come to take baths in what were said to be the healing waters.

Unfortunately, over time, the heat and humidity of the water had taken a toll on the interiors of the grand halls, and one by one they had closed their doors and been left to the ravages of nature.

They were too costly for the park service to renovate, and they sat idle for almost thirty years. But the community didn't want to lose the bath house heritage, so through a cooperative effort with the park service, local entrepreneurs had gotten involved and had so far saved three of the buildings. One had been re-purposed as an art gallery, one as a health spa and the other as a restaurant.

Abby was impressed with Grace's knowledge and asked, "Do a lot of people still come for the hot water? Do they really come to take baths?"

Grace nodded. "Yeah, a lot of people believe the hot waters do have healing properties. Doctors included. In fact, there was a time when doctors across the world would send patients here to take the baths. Famous people. Presidents, gangsters, baseball players, they all came.

"But not so much anymore. I've taken the tour but never really saw the point of paying to sit in a tub of hot water, especially with a bunch of strangers walking around.

"If it were like the old days and the springs were natural and outdoors and free, I might consider it. But with the water being piped in, I can't see paying fifty bucks for a twenty-minute soak."

I didn't say it out loud, but I agreed with her sentiment. Fifty dollars was a lot to pay for a few minutes in a bath tub filled with piped in water.

As we reached the end of Bath House Row, Grace pointed out the Arlington hotel and told about its long history of attracting the rich and famous. Al Capone, President Truman, and Bill Clinton stayed there when they were in town.

Leaving the Arlington behind, we passed a series of small shops and art galleries leading into an area known as Park Avenue. It was on the north end of Bath House Row and was originally where tourists had stayed in small motor courts. But after the big hotels were built, the motor courts closed and many went to ruin.

The area had seen some tough times, but it was clear that it was changing. A new coffee shop, a pizzeria, and a few art galleries had sprouted up and many of the quaint old buildings were being rehabbed.

Leaving Park Avenue, the road north took us back into the piney forests. Along the way, a road off to the right led to Gulpha Gorge, the National Park campground. I'd stayed there once before, and if I needed a place to camp in Hot Springs, it would be my first choice. But we weren't staying in Hot Springs; we were going to the crystal mine.

We were about six miles past the national park when Grace said, "If your friend came up here to dig crystals and if she didn't find what she wanted at Coleman's, she might have gone to another mine. There's one in Mount Ida that's known as having the best jewelry points. That's where the locals go when they want to find crystals they can sell.

"But your friend couldn't get there in a motorhome. The mine is six miles down a narrow dirt road and there's no campground. If she wanted to go there, she'd need to get someone to take her. But if she wanted to find crystals to sell, that'd be the place."

Abby was interested. "What's it called? This hard-to-get-to mine?"

"Sweet Surrender."

She touched the crystal hanging on the chain around her neck. "That's where I found this one, at the Sweet Surrender mine."

Chapter Nineteen

"Up ahead, on the right. Just past the greenhouses. Pull in there."

We had gotten to the junction of highway 5 and 7, just north of Hot Springs. Grace was telling me how to get to her brother's shop.

I slowed the motorhome and following her guidance, pulled off the road onto a driveway just past a row of greenhouses. A sign out front read, "Miller's Pit Stop, truck and car repair." The lot was small, but plenty big enough for the motorhome. I pulled in and parked.

The building looked like it had once been a gas station with two service bays. A glassed-in office on the right with a second story added above. That was probably where Grace lived.

A six-foot-high chain link fence separated the front lot from the back where several older cars and trucks were parked. Tall weeds sprouting between them suggested they had been there a long time, maybe even before her brother opened the shop.

On the front lot, to the left of the service bays, sat three green Jeep Cherokee wagons, each with a "For Sale" sign on their windshields. Next to the Jeeps, an older Dodge conversion van. It too had "For Sale" sign on it.

The door to one of the service bays was open, and I could see a car up on a lift with a man working under it. The office looked empty. No one inside.

As soon as I had the motorhome parked, Grace stood and said, "Don't go anywhere, I want you to meet my brother."

She grabbed her suitcase and hurried to the side door. She tried to open it but it was locked, and she couldn't get out. While she was standing there trying to figure how to unlock it, the man who had been working under the car turned and saw the motorhome. He nodded, pulled a rag out of his back pocket, wiped his hands, and started walking toward us.

He was about halfway across the lot when Grace finally got the door open. She stepped out, and the man's face lit up when he saw her. He ran over to her and said, "Grace, why didn't you call? I was worried."

Instead of waiting for an answer, he wrapped her up in a bear hug and said, "I'm glad you're back."

When he released the hug, he looked up at the motorhome and said, "Looks like you're riding in style. You want to introduce me to your friends?"

Abby had gone out the side door, closing it quickly behind her so that Bob wouldn't get out. I went out the driver's door and walked over to join her.

Grace made the introductions. "Walker, Abby, this is Daniel, my brother."

He smiled and shook our hands. He started to say something, but Grace interrupted. "They rescued me. Probably saved my life. They saw me on the side of the road and stopped to see if I was okay. I wasn't. They offered me food and water and a way to get back here. They were headed to the crystal mine in Jessieville. Going right by here. What are the odds?"

Daniel reached out to shake my hand again and said, "I really appreciate you bringing my little sister home safely. If there is anything I can do for you while you're in town, just let me know."

He turned to Abby and said pretty much the same thing to her. He then asked, "You drove all the way from Florida to come here to dig crystals?"

Abby shook her head and told him about Kat, that she was missing, and we had come to look for her. As the conversation continued, I turned my attention to the three Jeeps with the "For Sale" signs on them. They were older, probably 1999 or 2000 models, and looked to be the kind used by the US Forest Service.

Painted light green from bumper to bumper, and ordered from the factory without any luxury features, Forest Service Jeeps usually had cloth bench seats, a manual transmission, a six-cylinder motor and the all-important four-wheel drive. In the south, they might even have air conditioning, but not always.

Hearing Abby and Grace still talking behind me, I walked over to get a better look at the Jeeps. From thirty feet away, the baby Wagoneers looked pretty good. But as I got closer, I could see they showed signs of age—faded paint, cracked window glass, small dents, and sagging shocks.

Just as I was about to peek inside one, a voice behind me said, "I can make you a good deal on one of those if you're interested."

I turned to see that Daniel, Grace's brother, had walked over to join me. He looked to be about my age, thirty-five, and had the bearing of someone who, like me, had served in the military.

I pointed at the Jeeps. "Forest Service?"

He nodded. "Yep. Found them on an online government auction. Thought I was bidding on just one, but turns out I was bidding on a lot of three. When the transport showed up with three jeeps on it, I figured two were going to someone else, but they unloaded all three, gave me the titles and said they were mine."

I nodded. "They run?"

"Yeah, they do. One needs a clutch, but the other two are in pretty good shape. I've been going through the one closest to you. Replaced the belts and fluids, put in a new battery, did the brakes and shocks, and have a set of off-road tires I'm putting on this afternoon.

"If you're interested in it, I can make you a good deal."

I didn't need the Jeep because I had one back in Florida. A CJ that I could tow behind the motorhome. But still, the little green Cherokee was calling to me. It'd be fun to have one.

Before I could ask Dan how much he'd sell it for, Abby came over and said, "Hate to interrupt, but we need to get to the crystal mine and check in. We've got a lot of things we need to do before the day is over."

She was right. We needed to go to the mine and see if we could find Kat.

I told Dan I might call him later about the Jeep and he repeated his offer to give me a good deal. It'd be interesting to hear what he considered to be a good price. I knew what the Cherokee would be worth in Florida but didn't have a clue what it'd go for in Arkansas.

As we were walking back to the motorhome, Grace came up and handed me a map. "This shows the best places to dig crystals around here. Most are on logging roads near Jessieville. If your friend hooked up with a local, she might be digging at one of these spots.

"If she is, she might have hit a pocket and ended with a

bad case of crystal fever. That's when you get to a spot where you're finding really nice crystals and you just can't quit digging. I've seen it happen. Even to me.

"You get so caught up pulling crystals out of a pocket you totally lose track of time. You don't dare leave cause you're afraid someone will come in and get all the crystals you missed. So you end up staying. Sleeping in your car or whatever you've got.

"Since most of these places are way off grid, there's no cell service. No way to call and let people know where you are.

"If your friend has crystal fever, she's probably up in the hills, digging."

Grace pointed to a puddle at the far edge of the parking lot. "Could be she got stuck in the mud on one of those back roads. We get a lot of rain this time of year, and the roads turn to muck. Easy to get stuck when you get the fever and ignore the weather."

I knew about crystal fever. I'd experienced something like it when I was searching for gold coins on Florida's treasure coast. After my first big find, I didn't want to stop. Even with a major hurricane bearing down on me, I didn't want to quit digging. It almost cost me my life.

I also knew about getting stuck in the mud on dirt roads. When your tires sink down to the axle, you aren't going anywhere. At least not until someone comes along with a winch or a big four-wheel drive to pull you out.

If Kat were up in the mountains digging crystals, without cell service and stuck in the mud, it could take days to find her; assuming we had a four wheel drive vehicle and knew where to look. Hopefully it wouldn't come to that.

Grace stayed beside me as I walked back to the motorhome. When I reached the door, she said, "There's a

Walmart up ahead. You'll want to stop there and stock up. Get rubber boots and digging tools before you go to the mine. Get food if you don't already have some, cause they don't have any at the mine."

She leaned in and gave me a hug. "Thanks again for giving me a ride. You probably saved my life."

Then she whispered, "My phone number is on the back of the map. Call me before you leave."

Chapter Twenty

We left Grace and Daniel at their shop and headed north towards Jessieville and the crystal mine campground. It was still early afternoon and we had plenty of daylight left.

A few minutes after leaving, Abby said, "I saw you looking at the Jeeps. You want one, don't you?"

I shrugged. "I've got a Jeep back home. Don't really need another."

She laughed. "You didn't answer my question. You want one of those Jeeps, don't you?"

I did. But it didn't make sense to buy one and tow it a thousand miles back home. Still, I wanted one, so I said, "Yeah, I'd like to get one. They're like baby Wagoneers, little Jeep station wagons that can go almost anywhere."

She nodded. "They're four-wheel drive, right?"

"Yeah, four-wheel drive with a five-speed transmission and a six cylinder motor. The best combination."

She surprised me with what she said next. "You should buy one. We could use it while we're here and then you could sell it to me when we get back to Florida."

I looked over at her. "Sell it to you? Why would I do that? If I go to the trouble of hauling one back to Florida, I'm keeping it. Why would you want one anyway? They're almost twenty years old and have more than two hundred thousand miles on them. What would you do with one?"

She reached over and patted me on my knee. "Don't get snippy. If you don't want to sell me your Jeep, that's okay. I can get one on my own. As to why I'd want one, I live in the Keys. A little Jeep wagon would come in real handy down there. I could haul stuff in it, sleep in the back if needed, and the four-wheel drive would keep me out of trouble."

Her answer made sense, at least to someone looking for a reason to buy a Jeep Cherokee.

"I guess having a Jeep in the keys would be fun. Maybe after we get to the campground and check on Kat, we'll call Daniel and see what he wants for one."

Up ahead, I saw the sign for Walmart, and when we got close, I pulled in and parked near the gas pumps. After killing the motor, I turned to Abby and asked, "Did you hear what Grace said about getting rubber boots?"

She shook her head. "No, I didn't hear anything about rubber boots. I was too busy watching how she acted around you. How she tossed her hair and looked into your eyes. How she leaned in and got so close that I thought she was going to kiss you. So what'd she say that was so important?"

I ignored her jealous tone and said, "She said we should stop at Walmart and get rubber boots for the mine and we should get food cause they don't have any at the mine."

Abby crossed her arms. "Boots and food. You sure that's all she said?"

I nodded. "Yeah, boots and food at Walmart, that's all she said. She was just trying to be helpful."

Abby nodded. "I guess you're right. We probably do need to stock up on food, in case we have to stay longer than planned."

She stood, stepped over to the door and waited like she expected me to ask a question. She crossed her arms and looked at me. I was still sitting in the driver's seat, smiling like I had no clue. Finally I asked, "You want me to go into Walmart with you?"

She smiled. "Of course I do. You're supposed to be my husband on this trip. And that's what husbands do—go food shopping with their wife. So yeah, you're coming in there with me. But, because I'm nice, I'll let you push the cart.

"Now get up out of your seat, grab your wallet and let's go."

I smiled, got out of my seat, but instead of going to the door, I went to the back to check on Bob. I figured it wouldn't hurt Abby to have to wait a minute or two before I came back up front.

He was sleeping in his usual spot; the middle of my bed. I left him alone, washed my hands and headed back up front. Abby was waiting at the door and said, "I think you care more about that cat than you do me. I may have to see about changing that."

She winked and went out the door. I went out after her, locked up the motorhome, and we headed across the parking lot. Just your typical husband and wife going shopping at Walmart.

Thirty minutes later, with a shopping cart overflowing with food, supplies and a few non-essentials that Abby thought would make the RV feel more like home, we were back in the parking lot, heading for the motorhome.

It was mid-afternoon in November, and the fall weather in Arkansas was a welcome relief from the heat and humidity we'd left behind in Florida. The temperature was at least twenty degrees cooler than it had been when we left.

When we reached the motorhome, Abby went in and closed the bedroom door to keep Bob from escaping. Then she stood by the open side door while I handed her bags from the shopping cart.

I gave her the food first, which she put away while I unloaded the rest of the cart. Then, like a good shopper, I pushed the empty cart back to the nearest cart corral, safely out of the way of people coming in and out of the lot.

After putting everything away, Abby went back and let Bob out. He was waiting for me on the couch when I came in. He meowed once and ran back to the bedroom. He somehow knew we were getting ready to hit the road again.

According to our GPS, the Ron Coleman Crystal Mine was six miles north of where we were parked. I pulled out of Walmart and let the GPS guide me to the mine. Ten minutes later, we turned left onto Little Blakely road and followed it till the road ended at the mine entrance.

There was no doubt we were at the right place. Huge quartz crystal boulders lined the edge of the road leading to the mine office and store. Some of the crystals were the size of VW Beetles.

Outside the store, display tables were covered with crystals of all shapes and sizes, most with price tags attached. Visitors who didn't want to go into the mine and work up a sweat, could buy nice crystals at the store without getting their hands dirty.

Abby and I stepped inside the store and stopped at the cash register. The middle-aged woman behind it, having seen us arrive in a motorhome, asked, "You checking in?"

I answered. "Yes ma'am, we are."

When she asked our names, I hesitated, not knowing which ones to use, the real or the fake ones Abby had come up with. Seeing my hesitation, she said, "We're the Mendozas, Tony and Paige. We're the ones looking for our friend, Kat. You may have spoken with her father."

The woman nodded. "Ah yes, Kat's father. He's called several times wanting to know about his daughter. He said you two were coming to look for her, and he reserved you a site for a full week. He gave us his card and said to cover whatever expenses you had. Said whatever you needed, he'd pay for it.

"When he first called, he wanted you to have the site next to his daughter's, but it was already occupied. We had guests who had reserved it, and they didn't want to move. But for reason, they changed their plans; they pulled out this morning and the site is now yours.

She pointed out the window. "The campground is down there on the left. Pull in; drive around the first loop until you come to Kat's motorhome. The site next to hers is yours.

"It's a back-in site with full hookups. We don't have cable TV here, but you can usually pick up local stations with your antenna. The bathhouse is open 24 hours a day, no code required.

"Any questions?"

Neither Abby nor I had any.

The woman nodded and said, "If you need any help finding your friend, let me know. If you have a picture of her, I can post it in here. Maybe someone who knows where she is will see it."

I nodded. "Good idea. If we don't find her right away, we'll do that."

The lady smiled. "I'm sure she's okay. I wouldn't worry too much because we don't have much crime in these parts. Mostly pot smoking and drinking, nothing too serious.

"Your friend probably just met someone and is late

getting back. I'm sure you'll find her. But just in case, check the hospitals around Hot Springs. If she got hurt, she might be in one of them."

Back outside, Abby pulled out her phone and started making calls. There were three local hospitals, and she called them all. None had a record of Kat being admitted.

Chapter Twenty-One

We left the crystal mine store and headed to the campground. It was easy to find because the building at the main entrance was painted bright yellow and had the words, "Crystal Ridge RV Park" in tall, easy-to-read letters.

Rates were printed below the name. A full hookup site was twelve dollars a night. If you wanted to stay for a month, it was three hundred dollars. Either way, it was a bargain. Most campgrounds charge three times that.

To us, it didn't really matter what it cost since Kat's father was paying. Still, it was good to know the owners of the mine offered bargain rates to those who wanted to camp nearby. Owners of other parks weren't nearly so generous.

I pulled into the campground and took the first loop to the right. We stayed on it until we saw Kat's motorhome.

Parked next to it was an old Scotty travel trailer. Two-tone white with baby-blue accents. It looked to be a fourteen-footer. Small and compact.

Two rusted lawn chairs and a matching barbeque grill out front suggested more than one person stayed in the trailer. Toys scattered underneath along with a tricycle near the front door probably meant they had children. A collection of coffee can size crystals lined the ground between their trailer and Kat's, creating a border marking off their yard.

From the looks of it, the little blue Scotty hadn't moved in a long time. The tires were flat and several inches of pine needles covered the roof. An older gray Nissan Pathfinder was parked to the side, rusted fender wells all around and a good-sized dent in the left rear quarter panel. The right rear passenger window was covered with plastic and duct tape. A faded sticker with the words "Git-R-Done" hung from the rear bumper.

Judging from the chairs and toys and flat tires, it looked like the people staying in the trailer were full time residents of the campground, not day trippers or tourists. If that were the case; if they were there full time, they may have seen Kat, or even talked to her.

We'd have to check with them later. Maybe they knew something that would help us find her.

Kat's motorhome was in the next site over and just beyond it, the vacant one that had been reserved for us. Like the other sites we'd seen in the campground, ours had a level blacktop parking pad with a utility pedestal near the right rear corner. Tall oak trees on the back and sides provided a modicum of privacy, and could also make backing into the site a challenge.

I'd gotten a lot of practice backing into campsites since buying the motorhome and felt pretty confident I could get it in without any help. The backup monitor on the dash gave me a live video feed from the rear bumper, and let me see what was behind me.

Still, the campground loop road was narrow and there was no shoulder. If I misjudged my turn while backing in and dropped a tire off the edge, it might take a tow truck to get us back on solid ground.

Abby could tell I was a little concerned about getting into the site. She could see how narrow the road was and probably figured I might need help. She reached for the door and said, "Don't start moving until you see me in your mirror."

Being a man, I didn't need her help. I could have done it on my own. But not wanting to hurt her feelings and knowing it would be a lot easier backing in with her guiding me, I didn't stop her.

She got in position and using hand signals, got me into the site in one try. After she gave me a thumbs up followed by a "kill" signal, I turned off the motor and went out to join her.

She was standing at the back corner of the site admiring her work. When I walked up, she said, "So what do you think? Good enough?"

I nodded. "Yeah, good enough."

It didn't take an expert to see it was more than good enough. It was a text book parking job. Close enough to the power pedestal so hooking up was easy, but far enough from the trees for the slide room to go out without hitting them.

I pointed to the power pedestal. "I'll get us hooked up. You want to see how I do it?"

She shook her head. "Nope. I'll be inside waiting for you."

She didn't seem upset or anything, just not interested in seeing me pull out the power cord and connect it to the pole.

I guess if you've seen it once, there's no reason to stand around and watch someone do it again.

It took me less than five minutes to get us hooked up and when I went back inside, Abby was on the couch and Bob was up on the kitchen counter, looking out the window.

He knew he wasn't allowed on the counter, but sometimes he forgot. When that happened, I'd remind him it was off limits by pulling out the spray bottle I kept under the sink, and giving it a good shake. Usually, that's all it took.

He'd hear the water in the bottle and know that if he didn't get down, he'd get sprayed. So he'd jump down, and walk away in a huff. But sometimes, it'd take more than just shaking the bottle. Sometimes I'd have to actually spray him. And he never liked that.

The cool water from the bottle wouldn't hurt him, but he didn't like getting wet. So as soon as he saw the spray coming, he'd jump down and sulk off.

The spray definitely worked; it would get him off the counter, but neither of us felt good about it. I didn't like doing it and he didn't like getting wet.

He was still on the counter, so I grabbed the bottle and gave it a good shake to get his attention. He looked over at me, a sad expression in his eyes, but he didn't get off the counter. He just starred at me, flicking his tail back and forth.

It'd been a long trip for him, and he had to put up with the two strange women that had ridden with us. He was clearly stressed and didn't want to get sprayed. But he was up on the counter where we prepared our meals. His feet had been in his litter box and had touched his nightly deposits. Those same feet were up on the counter, leaving no telling what behind.

I shook the bottle again and was thinking about giving him a short spray when Abby came to his rescue. She got up off the couch, picked him up off the counter and started rubbing his head. She whispered, "Bob, the kitchen counter is off limits. You can go anywhere else, but not the kitchen counter. Understand?"

He didn't answer, but he did start purring. Maybe he understood what she was saying. Or maybe he just liked being held by a woman. Whatever the reason, he had avoided getting sprayed. He was off the counter and safe in her arms.

With Abby holding Bob, I figured it was a good time to run the slide out. It had lots of moving parts, and I didn't like the cat running free while it was moving. With him safely in her arms, I pushed the magic button that set the wall behind the couch in motion.

When it finally settled in its fully out position, Abby, with Bob still in her arms, took a seat on the couch. She seemed relaxed and in no hurry to check on Kat's motorhome. She patted the space beside her and said, "Have a seat."

I shook my head. "I don't want to sit. I've been driving all day and had plenty of sit time. What I want to do is to find Kat. I'm going to start by checking out her motorhome. You coming?"

I reached for the door and waited for her answer. I expected a "Yes," but that's not what I got.

Instead, she said, "No. We're not going over there yet. It'll be better if we wait. Come sit by me and I'll tell you why."

We'd driven over a thousand miles to reach Kat's motorhome, and I couldn't see any reason not to immediately go check it out. But Abby persisted. "Don't go over there. It'll be better if we wait a few minutes. Trust me."

I was still standing by the door, tempted to go out and check Kat's RV on my own. But something about the way Abby had said to trust her gave me pause. Maybe she knew something I didn't. Maybe her 'gift' was telling her we should wait. Maybe that was it.

I decided not to push it. I walked away from the door and sat down on the couch beside her. She patted me on the knee and said, "Don't worry; we'll go over there in a few minutes. In the meantime, just relax."

Yeah, right. Relax while sitting next to a woman who could read minds, see the future and come up with the winning numbers in a game of chance.

She probably knew what I was thinking. I was even more sure of that when she patted me on the knee again and said, "Relax. And, no, I can't read minds."

Chapter Twenty-Two

I had dozed off. The last thing I remembered was Abby telling me to relax. I didn't want to relax, but when she placed her hand on mine, calm had come over me, and I had gone to sleep.

The pop, pop sound of a small two-stroke engine had woken me. At first I thought it was a chainsaw in the distance, maybe someone cutting firewood. But the volume wasn't constant. It was getting louder. Whatever it was, it was coming our way, getting closer and closer.

I figured it was a motorbike. You see a lot of them in campgrounds. People with big RVs haul them around so they can get out and explore. Usually, they carry the newer and quieter bikes, the kind that won't disturb other campers.

The one I was hearing was louder than it needed to be and would definitely disturb other campers. Just as I was about to get up and see if I could see it, Abby tapped me on the leg and said, "Go ahead, take a look."

It was spooky how she seemed to know what I was thinking. No matter what it was, she knew. It was starting to get weird. But at that moment, it didn't matter; I was getting up anyway. I went to the window and looked out.

I was right about it being a motorbike. It looked to be an old Honda Trail 90, or a cheap imitation of one. Mustard yellow and leaving a long trail of blue smoke in its wake, it sounded like it was on its last legs.

I watched as the bike struggled to get up the hill leading into the campground, the trail of blue smoke thickening behind it. The rider, who was wearing a pair of oversized army surplus aviator goggles, a matching army surplus field jacket and dirt-covered camo pants, took the first loop into the campground and headed in our direction.

When he got to the trailer next to Kat's, he pulled in and parked. He got off the bike, unstrapped a black plastic egg crate filled with white rocks from the back and carried it to the trailer's front door.

Setting the crate down, he unlocked the door and went inside, leaving his collection of rocks on the deck.

From behind me, Abby asked, "That was him, right? The guy living in the trailer next to Kat."

I nodded. "Could be. He had a key and went in like it was his place."

She stood. "Good. That's what I was hoping for. I'm going to change clothes, and then we can go look in Kat's RV."

She headed back to my bedroom where she kept her clothes.

The temps were in the eighties when we left Florida, cutoffs and T-shirt weather, but we'd driven almost a thousand miles north. Being late November, the fall weather had taken hold. Highs in the low sixties, lows in the forties. A lot cooler than Florida.

I figured the chill in the air was the reason she wanted to change clothes; to get into something warmer, maybe jeans and a sweater.

I was right about the jeans but wrong about the sweater. When she came up front, she was wearing an almost see through low-cut tank top, white, no bra, showing lots of

130

skin.

I tried not to stare but failed miserably. She noticed and said, "You have a problem with the way I'm dressed?"

I shook my head. "No, not at all. In fact, I'm all for it. As long as you don't mind being cold, wear whatever you want."

She smiled. "Thank you, I'm glad I have your approval. Now it's your turn. Go change."

I was wearing the same thing I'd had on when we left Vicksburg earlier in the day; shorts and a lightweight shirt. Not ideal for the cooler temps in the mountains, but I was a man. I could handle it.

When I hesitated, she said, "Go change. Put on long pants and a sweatshirt. You'll thank me later."

She was doing it again. Pretending to know the future. Pretending to know that I'd be cold if I didn't change.

Rather than argue, I went back to my bedroom. Her clothes were carefully hung in my closet. Mine had been folded into neat piles and stacked on the floor. Her doing. A pair of my jeans and a gray sweatshirt had been laid out on the bed. She had picked out what I was going to wear and somehow, she'd gotten it right. She found my favorite jeans, well-worn and comfortable, and same with the sweatshirt. Both were what I would have chosen if she hadn't picked them out for me.

I dropped my shorts, pulled on the jeans and grabbed the sweatshirt. I was pulling it over my head as I headed back up front where Abby was waiting for me.

She nodded her approval but didn't say anything about what I was wearing. She walked to the door and said, "Let's go."

We went outside and over to Kat's RV. Hers, like mine,

131

was a Class C, which meant it was built on a cut-away truck chassis. It still had the driver and passenger doors up front in the cab, and another side door on the passenger side of the coach.

I tried the driver and passenger front doors first, but both were locked. The same was true with the coach door. It was locked as well. I would have been worried if they hadn't been. Being locked meant Kat had the time and presence of mind to secure them when she left. A good sign for her. But not for us.

With the doors locked, we couldn't get in. We wouldn't be able to see if Kat left a note or anything that could tell us where she was.

I turned to Abby. "Doors are locked. What do you suggest?"

She smiled and said, "Wait here." Then she walked around to the other side of the RV. I couldn't see what she was doing, but I could hear her open one of the lower compartment doors then close it a few moments later.

When she came back, she held up her hand and showed me a key ring that had four keys on it. "I'm pretty sure we can get in with these."

One of the keys had a Ford logo, which meant it probably opened the front door. I pointed to it and said, "That one. Let me try it."

She twisted it off the ring and gave it to me. I tried the front passenger door first, and with a simple twist, the key unlocked it. I pulled the door open and started to go in, but Abby stopped me. She grabbed the back of my sweatshirt and said, "I'm going in first. You wait out here for a minute."

She climbed in over the passenger seat and headed to the back of the motorhome. I stood outside for a few moments, and then without waiting for her permission, followed her in.

I wasn't sure what I was expecting, but what I found surprised me.

Chapter Twenty-Three

There were no dead bodies inside and no signs of a struggle. It was surprisingly clean. It did look like it had been recently traveled in, but nothing suggested any kind of foul play. No clothes thrown about. No broken furniture, nothing askew. The floors appeared to have been recently swept and there was no trash in the trash can.

It looked like Kat had cleaned up before she left.

The only odd thing was the cell phone sitting on the kitchen counter near the sink. Abby saw it and picked it up. She showed it to me. "Does this look like Kat's?"

I'd seen Kat's phone before. From what I could remember, it was a black Samsung Galaxy; no case and nothing about it that made it stand out or would identify it as belonging to her.

That was the way she liked things. Low profile. No "look at me" clothes; no fancy "rob me" jewelry; no bejeweled phone that someone would want to steal or remember as being hers.

She preferred a plain black phone. Like the one Abby had found on the counter. She was still waiting for me to answer her question, so I gave it my best shot. "Yeah, it's probably hers. See if it'll power up."

She pressed the button and waited for the vibration that would tell her the phone was coming to life. But there was no response.

She tried a second time, this time holding the power button down for ten seconds. Again, no response from the phone. She shook her head and said, "It's dead. We'll have to recharge it before we can see what's on it."

On the counter behind her, she found the charger plugged into a wall outlet. She connected it to the phone and waited until the charging light came on. Then she put it down on the counter and headed toward the back bedroom.

Kat's motorhome had the same basic floor plan as mine, a mid-kitchen with a dinette, a bedroom in the back, and a bathroom to the right of the bedroom.

Kat checked the bedroom first and saw that the bed was made. A little wrinkled, suggesting someone might have been napping on it before they left; nothing unusual about that. She then checked the closet and saw Kat's clothes hanging neatly inside. Shoes arranged on the floor, everything in order.

Next, she checked the bathroom. As with the bedroom, everything was where it was supposed to be. No sign of anything amiss.

While Abby was doing this, I checked the driver's area, looking for any clues to Kat's disappearance. There were no notes, no blood, no money, no credit cards. But there was a Garmin GPS sitting on the dash. I had one just like it in my RV and knew that it kept track of the roads it had been on, and where it was programmed to go next.

Hers wasn't plugged into the power port on the dash, which was good because if her motorhome were like mine, the outlet would be powered even when it wasn't running. Not a problem if you're driving, but if left plugged in for a long time when the motorhome wasn't in use, it could drain the battery. Kat probably knew this; that's why she had unplugged the GPS.

Even unplugged, it would retain information about previous routes and travel stops. I wanted to see those, so I plugged it in and powered it up. I went to the menu and had it show me the most recent travel route. It took a few seconds to pull it up, but it was still there.

There were no surprises. Kat had traveled from the same casino campground we had stayed in Vicksburg to the campground at the crystal mine. No route deviations, no travel since arriving.

I powered the GPS off and unplugged it from the power port. Like Kat, I didn't want to leave it plugged in and risk her returning to a dead battery.

Still up front, I looked around and noticed a bit of red clay on the floor mats on both the passenger's and driver's side. This suggested two people had gotten in the motorhome after digging in the crystal mine.

I called back to Abby. "You find any boots or digging tools back there?"

She came up front. "Sorry, I couldn't hear you. What was the question?"

I asked again. "You find any boots or digging tools back there? The kind they would use in the mine."

She thought for a moment then shook her head. "No, no tools, no boots. You know what that means?"

I had a pretty good idea what it meant, but I wanted to see if Abby thought the same thing.

She said, "It means they left here planning to go crystal mining. Now all we have to do is find out where they went and why they haven't come back."

She turned to the phone on the counter. "It was totally

dead. Probably take at least thirty minutes before we can get into it. We'll have to come back later."

She pointed outside. "Look."

The man who'd gone into the trailer next to Kat's had come back outside. He was no longer wearing aviator goggles or the surplus field jacket and we were able to get a better look at him.

He was probably in his late thirties, around five foot five, and skinny. Spiked black hair up front with a gray streaked mullet in the back. The faded blue Molly Hatchet t-shirt he was wearing could have been worth something to a collector had it not been oil stained. His ragged camo pants and dusty, work boots suggested he might work in the crystal mine. Maybe full time.

We watched as he walked over to his bike, lifted his arms high in the air and stretched. His T-shirt rode up giving us a clear view of his white belly. Had he been facing the other way, we would have probably been graced with a view of his butt crack. Fortunately, we weren't.

He looked around to see if anyone was watching and then bent over and picked up a rock off the ground. He examined it closely then shook his head and tossed it away. He turned and walked over to the tumble-down porch on the front of his trailer, crossed his arms and stared out toward to the crystal mine.

Abby put her hand on my shoulder and asked, "Shall we go meet the neighbor?"

Instead of waiting for my reply, she opened the door facing the trailer and stepped out. She took a few steps, waved at the man and called out, "Hey, how you doing?"

The man, not knowing that anyone else was around, turned to see who had spoken. When he saw Abby and how she was dressed, he smiled and said, "I'm doing well, especially now that you're here."

She was halfway over to his place before I stepped out. The neighbor was watching her and didn't notice me until I closed the door of the motorhome. He looked up at the sound and his smile instantly faded. He liked it better when it was just him and Abby.

Before he could ask, she said, "Yeah, he's with me. But don't let it bother you. We're here to have fun."

The man grinned. "Well, welcome to the neighborhood then."

He was looking at Abby when he said it and kept looking at her when I reached out to shake his hand. He grabbed mine, gave it a quick shake and let go.

All three of us were standing in front of his trailer. He was up on the deck, about a foot above us and we were on the ground in front of him. He had a great view down Abby's shirt and she knew it.

Looking at her, he asked, "You folks here to dig crystals?"

She nodded. "Yeah, we heard this was a good place to find them."

Still grinning and looking at Abby, he said, "This place ain't bad. You go over there to the mine, kick some dirt, and you'll find crystals. They won't be museum quality, but you'll definitely find them."

Abby smiled. "Good to know. But what if we want to find some really nice crystals, the kind we can sell? Where should we look?"

Before the man could answer, Abby stuck out her hand and said, "My name is Abby. What's yours?"

I was surprised she gave him her real name. She had done

the same with Grace and her brother Daniel. Maybe we were back to real names now. I'd have to ask her about it later.

The man grinned and took her hand. "Name's Byron, but everyone calls me Digger 'cause I'm the man you want to see when you're looking to dig the best crystals."

Abby smiled. "Really? You're the guy? So, if I want a crystal digging lesson, I come see you?"

He grinned. "Yep, I'm the guy. I can give you the best dang digging lesson you'll ever get."

The way he said it almost sounded dirty, kind of like he was coming on to her. I couldn't blame him if he was. She was wearing a nearly see thru top and almost throwing herself at him. Still, I wasn't sure I was comfortable with the way things were going.

He was still grinning when she said, "I'd like that, a digging lesson from you. But I got to find my friend first. Maybe you've seen her. Woman about my age, staying in the motorhome next to yours?"

The question took the wind out of Digger's sails. He wanted to talk more about giving Abby a digging lesson. That had real possibilities. Her changing the subject could derail his plan. Still, he didn't want to do anything that might hurt his chances with her.

He rubbed his chin like he was trying to think, then looked over at me and then back to Abby. He took a deep breath and said, "Yeah, I remember her. She showed up here last Thursday. Her and some guy. They spent all day Friday in the mine, but the guy she was with wasn't too happy with what they found. I offered to sell him some of my crystals, the really good ones, but he didn't want to spend the money."

Digger reached into his pocket and pulled out a flawless, six inch long, water clear quartz crystal with perfectly

140

formed points on both ends. He held it out for Abby to see.

"This is what the good stuff looks like. The kind of stuff I find. Museum quality."

Abby leaned in to get a closer look. Digger leaned in too, to get a better look at what was hiding under her tank top.

She looked up and asked, "Can I hold it?"

He grinned and said, "Yeah, but we might ought to sit down over there first. Don't want to risk you dropping it."

He nodded at the two lawn chairs in front of his trailer. Then he looked up at me. "You wouldn't happen to have any cold beer in that motorhome of yours, would you?"

I shook my head. "No, we're totally out."

Abby had already taken a seat in one of the lawn chairs and was waiting for us to come join her. She'd heard me tell Digger we didn't have any beer and, instead of staying quiet, she said, "A cold beer sounds good to me too. Why don't you go get us some?"

She was talking to me, playing some kind of mind game. She knew I wasn't going to unhook the motorhome and drive back to town to get beer, so I didn't know what she was thinking.

Digger moved over and sat down in the chair beside her. He was in her corner when it came to beer. He said, "They sell it down at Castleberry's Store. Corner of 7 and 298. Only about four miles from here. Maybe you could go over there and get us a twelve pack of Bud. Two twelve packs would be even better."

I could see that Abby was nodding in agreement. She liked the idea of me leaving her and Digger alone while I ran off to get beer. I was pretty sure she wasn't trying to make me jealous. We didn't have that kind of relationship. Not yet. So

I decided to play along.

"I guess I wouldn't mind going on a beer run, but I'm not taking the motorhome. Too much trouble to unhook and park it back in the site again. I can give you the money and you could go."

Digger rubbed his unshaven face, looked over at Abby in her low-cut top, then back at me. He reached into his pocket and pulled out a key. "I'll stay here with her, and you can take mine."

He nodded toward the Pathfinder parked next to his trailer. "It'll get you there and back, no problem. Just be light on the pedal 'cause it's nearly out of gas. The brakes are a little soft so give yourself plenty of time to stop. Other than that, it's fine."

I could see Abby nodding. She wanted me to go. She had a plan, and part of it meant I needed to leave. But I didn't like the way Digger was looking at her and wanted to stay close in case things got out of hand.

She could see my hesitation and said, "Walker, go get the beer. Don't worry about me. I'll be okay staying here with Digger. He'll keep me safe."

I looked in his direction, and he nodded. Still holding out the key, he said, "It'll only take you a few minutes. Go down to the highway, turn left, and you'll see the place about a mile down the road. Get two twelves of Bud. From the cooler."

I reluctantly took the key from him, even though I didn't feel right about going. Still, if Abby had a plan, and it meant I needed to be gone for a few minutes, I'd do it. For her.

I started to leave, but she stopped me. "You're going to need money."

She stood and turned to Digger. "We'll be right back."

She led me over to our motorhome and as soon as we were out of Digger's sight, she whispered, "Give me about twenty minutes alone with him, then come back. If you run into trouble, call me. You have money?"

I had my wallet, so yeah, I had money. I nodded.

"Good, take Digger's car, get the beer and come back. Don't get lost. Twenty minutes, that's all I need."

I wasn't totally convinced. "Abby, you sure about this? Leaving you alone with Digger, it doesn't feel right."

She smiled. "Don't worry, I've got this. Now go."

She kissed me on the cheek and pushed me away. We walked back over to Digger's and saw that while we were gone, he'd put on a different shirt and combed his hair, obviously wanting to make a good impression with Abby.

She headed for the chair next to his and I headed for the Pathfinder. The door was unlocked and I climbed in. I wasn't surprised the floorboard was caked in red clay from the nearby crystal mine but was surprised by the silver crucifix hanging from the rear-view mirror. Maybe Digger was religious. I hoped so.

I looked back to where they were sitting just in time to see him pull Abby's chair closer to his. He looked over his shoulder and gave me a thumbs up and a toothy grin.

The Pathfinder wasn't the worst vehicle I'd ever been in, but it was close. The windshield had a diagonal crack running from the top of the driver's side to the bottom of the passenger's. The driver's seat was ripped, the armrest on the door was missing, the headliner hung down like a sail, and there was an empty can of brake fluid on the floor.

When I turned the key to start the motor, the check engine light, the ABS warning light, and the low fuel light lit up and stayed lit even after the motor was running. I shifted into reverse and heard the transmission clunk as it tried to find a gear. I tapped the gas and was relieved when the car lurched backwards. At least reverse worked.

Out on the road, I shifted into drive and again felt the transmission clunk as it searched for matching gears. Being fairly certain the clunk meant I was in drive, I gave it gas and headed out toward the highway, leaving Abby and Digger behind.

Chapter Twenty-Four

My biggest mistake was believing Digger when he'd said there was enough fuel to get to the store and back. Instead of listening to him, I should have believed the flashing warning light on the dash. It was telling me I was about to run out of gas. The gauge said the same thing; the needle was pointing to the wrong side of empty.

I'd gone little over a mile when the engine stumbled. At first, I figured it was cold and just needed to warm up. I punched the gas, and it ran fine until I was about halfway through a right-hand curve. The engine stumbled again. A cough, then no power. It came back to life on the straight-away but stumbled a third time on the next right hander.

I pumped the pedal, trying to keep the motor going, but it didn't help. It died, and the rest of the warning lights on the dash lit up. The Pathfinder was out of gas.

I shifted into neutral and let it coast. It was mostly downhill to the highway and I figured if I got that far, I might be able to restart the engine and find a gas station nearby. Worst case, I could walk.

When I got to the highway, I lightly braked for the stop sign and not seeing any traffic, coasted on through taking a left. Up ahead about a quarter mile, like an oasis in the desert, I saw a sign for Wyles Kwik Stop. A gas station right where I needed it to be, downhill all the way from the stop sign.

I coasted the Pathfinder up the pumps and put twenty dollars of gas in the tank. Seeing a beer sign in the store window, I went inside and bought two twelve packs of cold Budweiser.

Digger would be happy, beer and half a tank of gas on me. With the little Pathfinder fueled up and twenty-four cans of cold beer in the passenger seat beside me, I headed back to his trailer to see how he and Abby were getting along. Hopefully, they were both fully clothed and still outside sitting in the lawn chairs.

Getting back to the campground was easy. The Pathfinder's check engine and ABS lights were still lit, but the low fuel light wasn't. Wind whistled through the plastic covering the busted rear window and cold air streamed out of the heater vents. I was glad Abby had made me change into warmer clothes. Had I not, I would have been mighty cold. Maybe her 'gift' had told her I'd be taking a trip in Digger's broken-down SUV.

I'd been gone a little over twenty minutes when I got back to campground. I parked the Pathfinder where it had been parked before, grabbed the beer out of the passenger seat and headed to where I had left Abby.

As I got close, I noticed that Digger was no longer sitting in the chair next to her. He was squatting on the ground facing her, about five feet away, a row of crystals lined up in front of him.

When he saw me, he quickly stood and walked over. "You make it there okay?"

I nodded. "Yeah. No problem."

"Good. I was worried about the gas. Wasn't much in the tank."

"Yeah, I know. I put some in for you. You want to take

146

the beer?"

He took both twelve packs and headed to his trailer. He stepped up on the deck and went inside, presumably to put the beer in the fridge.

With him out of the way, I went over to Abby.

"So, how'd it go? You learn anything?"

She nodded. "Yeah, a lot. And just so you know, he was a perfect gentleman, especially after I told him about your time in the service. He wanted to know if you saw any action, so I told him about the time you took on those three guys and left them in the dirt. After that, he decided he was sitting a little too close to me, so he got up and moved over there by those rocks."

She pointed to the row of crystals Digger had set up in front of her. "He was telling me about phantoms when you drove up. It's real interesting."

Behind me, I heard Digger coming back out of his trailer. He was heading in our direction carrying six beers. He handed one to me, another to Abby, and kept one for himself. He put the other three on a flat rock in front of us.

The chair he had been sitting in was empty. I waited to see if he was going to take it, but he didn't. Instead, he said, "You sit by the lady, and I'll sit over here by my rocks."

He plopped down, pulled the tab on his beer and took a long drink. When he was done, he wiped the foam from his lips with the back of his hand and said, "Now that there is some good beer."

He put the can down on the ground in front of him and pointed to one of the crystals he had lined up in front of Abby. It looked like a chunk of glass about the size of a pill bottle. One end was pointed and the other end jagged.

He picked it up and said, "This here is a busted point. It has nice size and clarity, but it's been broken, probably by a digging tool. The damage hurts its value. The people who buy healing crystals want them to be all natural and unbroken. Not like this. Rocks like these are only good for yard art and aquariums."

He picked up the rock beside it; it was much larger, flat on the bottom with a lot of tiny crystals on top. "This here is a cluster. Has a rock base with lots of crystal points growing out of it. Clusters like this come in all shapes and sizes, some as small as a quarter, some larger than a car. They got one up there at the welcome center probably weighs twenty tons.

"You'll find clusters just about everywhere in these hills. Most won't be jewelry or collector quality, but some will be. Look for ones with unbroken points. Those are the keepers."

He set the cluster down and picked up a crystal about the size of a cigar. When he handed it to Abby, he said, "That there is a phantom. If you hold it up to the light, you'll see the ghost of another crystal inside."

Abby held it up and said, "Yeah, I see what you mean. It looks like another crystal growing inside it."

She showed it to me, and I saw the ghost image of the crystal inside the big one. I nodded and had to admit it was pretty cool. Abby took the crystal back and handed it to Digger.

He carefully wrapped it in a tissue he pulled from his pocket and gently put it on the ground next to the others. He pointed at it and said, "People who believe crystals have healing powers, cherish phantoms. If you ever find one, keep it forever."

He bent over and picked up another crystal about the same length of the phantom, but a bit thicker. He handed it to Abby and said, "Tilt it to one side. Tell me what you see."

She held the crystal vertically with her thumb and forefinger, then slowly rotated it until it was horizontal. Something caught her attention and she leaned in to get a closer look. She shook her head and repeated the rotation. Then she looked up at me with surprise in her eyes and said, "There's water in it!"

Digger nodded. "There sure is, and that water is millions of years old; probably got there back when dinosaurs roamed this part of the world."

Abby showed me the crystal, and when she tilted it, I could see the water trapped inside. It moved like the bubble on a carpenter's level. Clear liquid, maybe half an ounce.

Digger waited until we looked back up at him, then said, "We call them 'hydros'. They're rare, but they do exist. I found that one about six miles from here."

He took the hydro from Abby and put it back on the ground next to his other crystals. He picked up another one but kept it hidden in his hand until he was close enough to Abby to reveal it with a bit of flair.

With the crystal still hidden, he said, "This is one of my prized possessions. I almost cried the day I found it."

He opened his hand and revealed a clear quartz crystal with what looked like blades of grass embedded inside.

Abby leaned in to get a closer look. She stared at it for a moment then looked up at Digger with wide eyes. "Is it real?"

He nodded. "You bet it is. And rare too. We call that green stuff an inclusion, something that got caught inside the crystal while it was growing. Inclusions can be almost anything. Dirt, minerals, even bits of grass or leaves."

"I've found a few inclusions in my life, but this is the one I like best. Never seen another like it."

He showed it to both of us but didn't let us hold it. I guess it was too rare or valuable to risk putting it in our hands. When we had seen enough, he wrapped the crystal in tissue and put it in his shirt pocket.

Then he pointed to the remaining crystals laid out in front of him. "These are the kinds I look for, the really special ones, the kind most people who dig all their lives will never find. But I find them because I know where to look."

Abby nodded. "That's some pretty amazing crystals you got there. Probably worth a lot of money."

Digger leaned back, taking the compliment in full. He obviously liked it when people praised his collection. He took a drink from his beer and said, "I showed all these to your friend, the gal who showed up in the motorhome next door."

Abby nodded. "What'd she think about them?"

"She liked them, so much so that she begged me to show her where she could find others like them."

He grinned but said nothing else.

Chapter Twenty-Five

We waited for Digger to tell us the rest of the story about what happened after he showed Kat his collection of crystals. But instead of talking, he popped the top on another beer, leaned back and just nodded.

It was clear he was waiting for us, or, more specifically, Abby in her low-cut top, to beg him to tell us more.

When it became apparent that he wasn't going to say anything unless she asked, she took the bait. "Digger, did you show Kat where to find crystals?"

He didn't answer right away. He was sitting on the ground in front of the crystals lined up in front of him, seemingly mesmerized by what he was seeing. He didn't look up in response to Abby's question.

She asked him again, this time a little louder. "Digger, did you show Kat where to find crystals?"

This time he heard the question. He looked up at Abby and started nodding. Then he pointed over his shoulder and said, "Back during World War II, the government needed quartz crystals. Not just regular crystals. They needed to be oscillator grade to use in radar and guidance systems.

"But there were only a few places in the US where they could be found. One of them was here in these mountains. They sent in a survey team, and after a few weeks of hunting, they found the mother lode—a place packed with high quality oscillators.

"Back then, there were so many crystals on the mountain, you could just pick them up off the ground. Cigar size and bigger. The locals knew about them, but to them they were just fancy rocks. Yard art or trinkets to put on the window sill.

"But to the government the crystals meant the difference between winning or losing the war. As soon as the site was located, President Roosevelt signed a bill making about half a million acres around the mother lode a protected national forest.

"Not many people lived in those woods back then, and no one really cared what the government did as long as it would shorten the war. Of course, no one knew the government was taking all that land just to get to the crystals.

"Anyway, the Army came in, bulldozed a road to the site and set up a small camp. They kept a team of geologists up there digging crystals for the rest of the war.

"Later on, the government scientists figured out how to grow oscillators in their labs and didn't need to dig them out of the ground anymore. So they abandoned their dig site up on the mountain and erased all mention of it in their records.

"Fifteen years later, when the Forest Service started mapping the area, they had to come up with names for all the mountains. Most of them, they just made up. But one of the fellas doing the mapping remembered the dig site where the Army had found crystals, and he named that site Crystal Mountain.

"It don't show up like that in any road map because there aren't any paved roads going to the place. But if you get a GS topo map and know where to look, you'll see a spot labeled

Crystal Mountain.

"If you go up there and know where to look, you can still find the best crystals on the planet. The army only took a small fraction of what was there, they left most of them behind."

Digger was nodding while he was telling the story, never looking up, just staring at his rock collection.

When it was clear he had nothing more to say, Abby asked, "Did you tell Kat about Crystal Mountain? Is that where she went?"

Instead of answering, he took a final slug from his now warm beer and reached over to get another one. He looked up at me and asked, "Beer?"

I shook my head. I didn't want another beer. I wanted to find out where Kat was.

When he asked Abby if she wanted one, she said, "No, but you go ahead. You've earned it."

He grabbed a beer and felt the side of the can. "They're getting warm. Okay if I go inside and get a cold one?"

Abby looked in my direction like she wanted me to answer, so I did. "No need to drink warm beer when there's cold ones inside. So yeah, go ahead, get you one."

Digger stood, grabbed the empty beer cans and went back to his trailer, leaving the door open behind him. We heard him drop the empties into what we assumed was a trash can, followed by the distinct sound of him in the bathroom, peeing. That was followed by running water (we hoped he was washing his hands) and then the sound of drawers being opened and paper being shuffled.

A few minutes after he had gone in, he returned with a sheet of paper in his right hand and beer in his left.

He sat on the ground in front of his crystal collection and took a sip of his beer. Then he cleared his throat, looked up at me and tapped the sheet of paper in his hand.

"There's a place on Crystal Mountain that only a few people know about. People whose daddies were there during the war. Most of them are too old to dig. Their memories of the exact location of the site have faded, and it's not being passed on to their kids.

"But an old soldier took me up there and showed me where the army had been digging. He called it the Crystal Cave, a hole in the mountain where double terminated crystals could be plucked from clay walls. The cave floor was littered with crystals of all sizes, some with inclusions, some with hydro. All of them valuable."

"I told Kat about this secret place. I probably shouldn't have, but I did. I told her about all the crystals that could be found up there; about how you didn't even need to dig for them. You could just pick them up off the ground."

"I shouldn't have told her. I shouldn't have shown her the same crystals I showed you because it built a fire inside her. Something she wouldn't be able to quench until she went up there to see for herself.

"The guy she was with, he didn't believe me. He said there was no such place as the Crystal Cave or Crystal Mountain. No place where you could go and just pick up museum quality crystals right off the ground.

"I told him he was wrong. Crystal Mountain was real. So were the crystals you could find there."

He laughed at me, and he laughed at your friend when she said she believed me. They argued, and he said he was leaving. Said he'd be back to get his stuff later on. He walked to the road, stuck out his thumb and got a ride from one of the Rainbow people.

That was Saturday, lots of people coming and going at the mine. I was here most of the day and didn't see him come back.

Digger paused for a minute then said, "Your friend, Kat? She seemed relieved the guy was gone. Didn't shed a tear about his leaving. She sat right there where Abby's sitting and said she wanted to know more about Crystal Mountain. Because she believed me."

He took a long sip from his beer. His throat parched from talking so much. Abby and I wanted him to continue, to tell us more about Kat. We didn't want to give him any excuse to end his story, so we made no move to leave.

After about a minute of silence, he put his beer can on the ground and tapped the sheet of paper he had brought out of his trailer. "I shouldn't have told her how to get to Crystal Mountain. Not on that day. Rain was in the forecast, and the dirt roads up there can get pretty messy.

"But she wanted to know. She even offered me money to draw her a map. I felt bad about taking money from her, but I was broke and needed it to pay some bills. So I made her a map and showed her how to get there.

"I told her it was dangerous to go alone. Told her she'd need four-wheel drive. But she didn't listen.

"Later that same day, a guy showed up at her campsite driving one of them little Korean cars. Said it was a rental she had ordered.

"Next morning, she locked up her motorhome and drove off in that little car. By herself. That was Sunday. As far as I know, she hasn't been back since. I was in court Monday, so if she came back then, I missed her."

He tapped the piece of paper he had been holding.

"I don't know if she went up to Crystal Mountain or not. Maybe she did or maybe she went off after her boyfriend. I don't know. I do know it rained hard Sunday afternoon and again Sunday night. If she was up there in that rental car, she probably got stuck in the mud.

"But maybe not. Maybe she went to Hot Springs and found her boyfriend. Could be they got a room at the Arlington and are taking those hot water baths. That's what all the tourists do."

He paused and took another sip of his beer. Then he lowered his head and said nothing. Again, he was waiting for us to ask the next question. The question he knew we had to ask.

Abby didn't wait long. She pointed at the sheet of paper in his lap. "You drew a map for her. Is that what you've got there, a map to Crystal Mountain?"

He looked up from his beer, pretending to be ashamed of what he was about to say. But he said it anyway. "Yeah, it's a map showing how to get to Crystal Mountain and the Crystal Cave. But I can't give it to you. It's too valuable to give away, especially since I need money to buy food and pay bills."

Abby nodded. "I understand. The map is real valuable. But we're not going up there to look for crystals. We just want to find our friend."

Digger shook his head. He was holding firm.

"It don't matter whether you're going up there to dig or not. This map is too valuable to give away for free. Only a few people know about Crystal Mountain or how to get there, and I want to keep it that way. That's why I don't give the map away to anyone. Not for free."

I'd had enough of his talk. I pulled out my wallet, opened

it and asked, "How much?"

Chapter Twenty-Six

He didn't answer right away. He looked at the map and shook his head. "People who make a living digging and selling crystals would be happy to pay big bucks for this map. It shows them exactly where to go to get museum quality specimens. The kind they can sell for top dollar. It's hard to put a price on something like that."

I figured Digger already had a price in mind and he was just baiting us, hoping that when he told us the amount, it'd sound reasonable. Or maybe he was hoping I wouldn't wait for his price and I'd make an offer. He saw the motorhome we were in. He had to figure we had money.

But I didn't fall for it. I didn't offer anything. Instead, I repeated the question I'd asked before. "How much for the map?"

He looked down at the sheet of paper, rubbed his nose and looked back up at me. He smiled and said, "Just for you, because you said you wouldn't be digging any crystals, a hundred dollars."

The price surprised me. A hundred dollars was a lot of money for a hand-drawn map that may or may not be worth anything.

But Digger had already given us more than the map. He had told us about Kat's movements from the time she arrived in camp until she disappeared. He told us about her boyfriend leaving and the car she rented, and maybe where she took it to dig crystals.

If I paid him his asking price for the map, he might be willing to tell us more, he might even agree to keep an eye on Kat's RV when we couldn't. So, without trying to bargain him down, I reached into my wallet and pulled out five twenties. I handed them over, and he gave me the map.

I thought it would be a hand drawn original, but it wasn't. It was a copy of something that had been created on a computer. The top half of the page had a map from Google, with a tent icon marking our location in the campground. From there, a jagged line led across the map to a large X.

Below the map, the following instructions.

```
From Castleberry's store, go north on
highway 7 for six miles until you see
the national forest sign for FR 132.

Turn right at the sign onto the dirt
road and stop.

Reset your trip odometer to 0.0.

Go east on the dirt road for 3.7 miles
and go left at the fork. At 4.8 miles,
go right.

Keep going east until your trip
odometer shows 13.3. Don't turn, keep
going straight.

Just before the 14-mile point, there
will be a wide spot on the right side
of the road. Pull over and park there.

Get out and cross the road to your
left. Look up the hill. There won't be
a marked trail, but if you look
closely, you'll see a narrow path going
```

```
up.

Follow the path for about sixty feet
until you see a white quartz
outcropping.

Follow the base of the outcropping to
the east (your right) until you reach
the Crystal Cave.

It's a hand dug mine, not a cave. When
you see it, you'll recognize it.
```

Whoever had created the map had been precise. Every turn and bend had been noted. If it were accurate, it would make it easy to find Crystal Mountain and the Crystal Cave, but only if they really existed.

I had to wonder, though, since the map was obviously a copy and easily duplicated, how many had he sold and at what price?

Was the story he told us the same one he told to every tourist who showed up at the campground? Did they all buy copies of the map from him?

I handed it to Abby and looked at Digger. I crossed my arms and asked, "How many copies have you sold?"

He smiled nervously. "Not many. Maybe twenty."

I nodded, not sure I believed him. Then I asked, "When was the last time you were up there, at the Crystal Cave on Crystal Mountain?"

He shook his head and looked over at his Pathfinder. "Been a few months. Truck broke down last time I tried to go. I don't trust it to make the trip no more."

Having driven it, I could believe it broke down on him. It almost broke down on me, and I'd only gone a few miles. I nodded and asked, "So if I get something reliable to get us up there, you going with us?"

Instead of answering right away, he looked down at his feet. Then he looked up and said, "I can't go up there no more. They got a T.O. on me."

I was pretty sure I knew what a T.O. was, a Trespass Order. Usually filed by store owners to keep shop-lifters and trouble makers off their premises. I'd never heard of one being filed by the Forest Service.

"Tell me about the T.O."

Again, Digger looked down at his feet. When he looked back up, he said, "It weren't really my fault. I was up there with some friends, and they'd been drinking and had a fire going, and, well, it got out of hand. Burned about thirty acres before the rangers got it put out.

"They couldn't prove it was set on purpose, so they got our names and let us go.

"Next time I was up there, the guy I was with, he took a shovel and dug some pretty deep holes looking for crystal. The Forest Service, they don't allow you to dig holes. But this guy did anyway.

"He was about five feet down when the ranger walked up on us. They wrote both of us tickets and told us not to come back.

"Two weeks after that, I was up there again, this time with three other fellows. They had used a winch to pull this big crystal out of the ground and then up into the bed of their truck. On the way back down the mountain, they was smoking pot, not paying attention. We come around a curve and run right into the ranger's Jeep.

"No one was hurt. But the driver was ticketed, and we all got wrote up. Since there was damage to a government vehicle, we had to go to court.

"The Forest Service, having cited me four times within two months, asked the judge for a Trespass Order. The judge wrote it up and said I was lucky I was getting off so easy. He said next time I got caught up there, I was going to jail.

"That's why I can't go with you. If I go back up there and violate the order, I go to jail. I been in jail and don't want to go there again. So while I'd like to go up to Crystal Mountain with you, I can't. They'll arrest me."

Abby had been listening to his story and nodded like she believed him. But she had a question. "Digger, how many rangers patrol that part of the national forest?"

He squinted, thinking about the answer. I could see him counting numbers, whispering to himself. Finally, he said, "There's four of them that I know of."

She nodded. "And how big is the district?"

He grinned. "It's big. Take a day to drive from one end to the other. Runs from Mt. Ida all the way to Benton. Couple hundred square miles at least."

She smiled at his answer. "So they have four rangers covering two hundred square miles of forest roads. What makes you think they're going to find you if you go up there with us?"

He shook his head. "They'll find me because they'll be out in force watching them Rainbow people. Those hippies are camped out on the main road leading to Crystal Mountain. The rangers have checkpoints up and down that road and they stop every car; checking IDs, looking for drugs, guns and what not.

"I'm on their list. They stop us and find me; I get arrested. No way around it. And there ain't nobody going to bail me out. Not this time."

Abby nodded like she still believed him. She looked at me and asked, "Anything you want to ask him?"

"Yeah. Digger, you said Kat took off Sunday morning in her rental car. She talk to you before she left?"

He shook his head. "I usually don't get up that early, but that morning I did. I wanted to get over to the mine before it rained.

"I saw her putting a few things in the car, so I went over to talk. She didn't have much to say. Just that she was going to look for crystals and hoped it didn't rain before she got back."

I nodded. "So she *was* planning to get back that day? Sunday, right?"

He nodded. "That's what it sounded like. But she didn't come right out and say when she was coming back. Just that she was going to go look for crystals."

"You said she was putting things in the car. What kind of things?"

He shrugged. "I don't know. Just things."

Then he thought for a moment and blurted out, "Boots, I saw boots! And water, two six packs of bottled water. And jeans and a sweatshirt. Maybe a backpack."

I gave him a minute to see if he could remember anything else. But he didn't, so I asked, "It didn't bother you when she didn't come back Sunday evening?"

He shook his head. "Come Sunday evening I wasn't thinking too straight. A couple of buddies come over that afternoon, and because it was too wet to dig, we went inside and finished off a bottle of Old Crow. She could have come in with a marching band and I wouldn't have heard her."

I nodded. I had one last question. "Do you know who she

rented the car from?"

He shook his head. "No idea. They just came and delivered it. That's all I know."

We'd gone over to Digger's trailer around two in the afternoon. We'd been there two hours and gotten as much information from him as we figured we could. It was time to leave.

Abby stood first. She said, "Digger, we appreciate your help. If you think of anything else, let us know, okay?"

He nodded. "I will, I promise."

I stood and took Abby's hand. "We'll be next door if anything comes up."

We left his campsite, walked over to our motorhome, unlocked the door and went inside.

Chapter Twenty-Seven

Bob met us at the door with a howl. He wasn't happy we'd left him alone in a new place. But he was glad we were back. He showed it by closely following in our footsteps until we sat on the couch. Then he jumped up and joined us. He rubbed his body against my shoulder then moved over to Abby and settled down onto her lap.

We'd been gone half the afternoon, most of it spent listening to Digger tell us stories about Crystal Mountain. I wasn't sure whether they were true or not, but I was pretty sure he was in the business of telling the story to anyone who would listen so he could sell maps for a hundred bucks each.

I looked over at Abby. "What do you think? You think she went up there, to Crystal Mountain?"

She shrugged. "I don't know. His story sure made me want to go. If he did the same show and tell for her, she'd probably want to go there too."

I nodded in agreement. "So, we going up there?"

Abby moved Bob over to my lap and stood. She pointed to the back and said, "Before I do anything, I'm going to change into warmer clothes. Then I'm going over to Kat's to check her phone. It should be charged up by now.

"If it is, I'll see who she called about a rental and see if they can tell me where the car is. Some of those places have GPS trackers, makes it easier to find their cars if they get stolen.

"If we're lucky and find out where the car is, that's where we'll go next."

I nodded. "Sounds like a good plan. What do you want me to do?"

She didn't answer. Instead, she headed to the back. A few minutes later, she came up front wearing one of my gray sweatshirts. It was a bit too large, but somehow it looked good on her.

She stopped in front of the couch and said, "Don't do anything until I get back. If the rental company says Kat's car is up on Crystal Mountain, I'll see if we can rent something with four-wheel drive. We'll need it if we go up there looking for her."

She headed for the door but stopped before opening it. She asked, "You think of anything else I need to do while I'm over at Kat's?"

I nodded. "Yeah, leave her a note. Tell her we're looking for her and, if she shows up while we're out, to call us."

"Good idea. I'll do that."

She grabbed her phone and headed out. I stayed on the couch with Bob, mostly because he wasn't letting me up. Not without delivering some pain first.

He had been kneading my leg the way cats do, making donuts, pushing and pulling his paws against the fleshy part of my thigh. When he saw Abby heading for the door, his claws came out, pushing against my leg, claws in, claws out. He was telling me it would be in my best interest to stay with him for a bit, not to leave him alone again.

Since I didn't have any other plans and didn't want him to rip into my legs, I didn't get up. I sat there and petted him until he relaxed and retracted his claws.

Thirty minutes later, Abby returned. Phone against her ear. She was saying, "Yeah, that's a good price. Tell him it's a deal. But we want it tonight if there's any way possible.

She paused then said, "Great. We'll be here."

She ended the call, and, with a smile, asked, "Guess who I was talking to."

I could only think of one person who would bring a smile to her face. "Kat? Did you find Kat? Were you talking to her just now?"

She shook her head. "No, that wasn't Kat. She's still missing. But I learned a few things."

I was still wondering who she had been talking to, so I asked, "If that wasn't Kat, who was it?"

She smiled. "It was Grace. I called her about buying one of her brother's Jeeps, one of the green ones. We agreed on a price, and he's bringing it up here this evening."

I was surprised with her answer. "You bought a Jeep?"

She nodded. "I did. I'll tell you why in a minute. But first, let me tell you what I learned about Kat."

She came over and sat down beside me on the couch. Bob moved off my lap onto hers. Maybe hers was more comfortable than mine. Or maybe Bob just liked women more than he liked men. In any case, with Bob on her lap, she told me what she'd learned.

"Kat's phone was password protected. It took me about four tries before I remembered what it was. Casper. The name of the dog she had when she was a kid. I tried it, and it unlocked the screen.

"I checked her call log and saw she had a lot of incoming calls from me and you and her father. All unanswered. I went back a few days and found the outbound calls. The last one was to a car rental place in Hot Springs.

"I called them and they confirmed she had rented a car. When I asked if it had a tracker on it and if they could tell me where the car was, they said, 'No.' They wouldn't reveal the location of a customer's car without a court order.

"I explained we were worried our friend was stuck and needed help, but they still said, 'No.' They wouldn't tell me where the car was. But they did tell me something interesting.

"Day before yesterday, she brought the car back and swapped it for another one."

Abby paused to see how I'd respond to this revelation. She knew it was important.

"You know what that means?"

I nodded. "Yeah, it means two days ago she was alive and well in Hot Springs at the car rental place. That's good news."

Abby nodded. "It is. But she still hasn't come back here, and that's kind of worrisome. I called her father and let him know about the car rental and he was happy for the update but wondered where she was now.

"I told him about Crystal Mountain, and he said to go check it out, no matter what it cost or what we had to do to get there. I told him we would and I'd call him as soon as we learned anything new.

"I called the rental place back and tried to rent something with four wheel drive. But the closest they had was a front wheel drive Kia Soul and I didn't want to try to tackle the mountain in that.

"Then I called Grace. Told her I wanted to buy one of her brother's Jeeps. Told her it needed it to be roadworthy and ready to take us into the back woods. When she asked why, I told her we needed to get to Crystal Mountain, and she laughed.

"She said last spring she'd gone looking for Crystal Mountain and could never find it. The roads weren't marked and the map she had ended up getting her lost. She said if we were going out on those forest roads, we needed to take food, water and plan on not coming back anytime soon.

"We talked some more and then she put me on hold. When she came back, she said her brother would sell me the Jeep that was ready to go for thirty-five hundred dollars.

"I told her it was a deal if they could deliver it to our campsite. She said they could do that, and could probably have it up here in an hour."

I smiled. "Good move. Having the Jeep will make it easier for us to get around. But I wonder. If Kat had a rental car, why hasn't she come back to her motorhome? You'd think she'd at least come get her phone or a change of clothes or something. That's the part that bothers me. Why hasn't she come back?"

Abby rubbed her head. "Maybe she has come back and we just don't know about it. We're basing everything we know on what Digger told us. He said she left on Sunday and he hasn't seen her since. But that doesn't mean she hasn't been back. It just means Digger didn't see her if she did.

"She could have easily come and gone when he was sleeping or when he was out in the mines or off with his friends. She could have even spent last night in her RV. If she left early this morning, we wouldn't know. Just because Digger didn't see her doesn't mean it didn't happen.

"All we know for sure is she was at the car rental place two days ago. We don't know where she's been since."

Abby was right. Kat could have been back in her motorhome as recently as that morning and we wouldn't know it. We only knew what Digger had told us and it might turn out that he wasn't the most reliable source of information.

I changed the subject. "So, you bought a Jeep. Does that mean we're going to Crystal Mountain?"

She nodded. "Yep. We have to. We don't know if she is up there or not, but we have to go look. She might be up there stuck in the mud.

"If she is, she's smart enough to know her best chance of rescue is to stay with her car. Or maybe she's already been rescued, maybe by one of those Rainbow people. She could be safe and sound at their camp for all we know

"The thing is, we don't know if she went to Crystal Mountain. She could have picked up her boyfriend and they could be staying at one of those fancy hotels in Hot Springs and taking the baths.

"But if there is any chance she's stuck in the mud up on the mountain, we have to go look. Don't you agree?"

Before I could answer, there was flash of light followed by a clap of thunder.

A storm was moving in.

Chapter Twenty-Eight

"So, what do you think? We going up there tonight, to Crystal Mountain?"

Abby and I were sitting on the couch, listening to the heavy rain hammer down on the roof of the motorhome. She had asked the question, and I didn't know the answer. Not yet.

The problem was we didn't know where Kat was. We didn't know if she had gone up on Crystal Mountain or if she was sitting in a hot tub in Hot Springs. And even if she had gone to Crystal Mountain, we didn't know if she was still there or not.

What we did know was it was raining pretty hard and the dirt roads through the national forest would be slick. We knew it would be dark before we could leave and we knew we couldn't leave until Grace and her brother showed up with the Jeep. And we didn't know if the Jeep was up to the task of getting us to Crystal Mountain and back.

All we really knew was Kat was missing, and there was a slight chance she was up on Crystal Mountain.

I was thinking about this while Abby was waiting for my answer. The truth was I wanted to go look for Kat even if it meant heading out in the rain in an untried vehicle on muddy back roads. But I wasn't going to make the decision alone. So I asked her, "What do you think? You think she's up there?"

Abby had done a pretty good job of convincing me she could somehow sense future events. The money she had won at the roulette wheel by picking two winners in a row was either an amazing stretch of good luck or proof of some kind of gift.

If the roulette wins had been the only thing, I might have written it off as a fluke. But she'd somehow sensed Grace's presence at the abandoned gas station in Louisiana long before we got there. Plus she knew to wait at our campsite for our neighbor to ride up on his moped.

I had no idea how she was able to do these things but she had. It made me think that maybe she really did have some kind of gift.

If she did, I hoped it would help her sense Kat's present condition and whether she was in dire need of our help or not.

I was waiting for Abby to answer my question about whether she thought Kat was up on the mountain, but instead of answering, she closed her eyes and placed both hands on Bob's back, one on each side of his rib cage. He was in her lap and she had been petting him since she'd returned. He had purred continually during her pets. But when she put both hands around his back, his purring abruptly stopped.

I watched, expecting him to jump off the couch and run to the back. He didn't like to be touched that way. No two-handed holds for Bob. It was too restrictive, it made him feel trapped.

But he didn't run. Instead, he closed his eyes and put his head down between his front paws and appeared to go to sleep. Whatever Abby was doing, it didn't bother him. In fact, he seemed to like it.

They stayed like this for a long time, both with their eyes closed, heads down, appearing to sleep. I didn't know what Abby was doing. For all I knew, she could have been channeling with another dimension or just resting her eyes after a long day. Either way, I wasn't going to bother her or Bob.

After about twenty minutes, her eyes suddenly opened and she said, "They're here."

It was still raining outside, a steady drizzle. The thunder and lightning had passed, that part of the storm was gone. The drumming sound of the rain on the roof had been with us for about thirty minutes, loud enough that if we wanted to speak, we had to raise our voices.

But our conversation had ended when I'd asked Abby what her future sense told her about Kat's condition. She had closed her eyes and had said nothing.

She repeated herself. "They're almost here. You need to be ready."

She tapped Bob lightly at the base of his stubby tail. He opened his eyes, stretched and jumped down off the couch and headed straight to the back. He sensed we were about to have company and didn't want any part of it.

Abby stood and said, "I'm going to the back for a minute. Got to get something. When they get here, don't make them wait in the rain. Go out and greet them."

From the sound of tires on the wet gravel coming from outside, I knew she was right. We had visitors.

Looking out the front window, I saw two green Jeep Cherokees pull in and park in front of the motorhome. Grace got out of one, her brother Daniel got out of the other. They headed for the motorhome, and I met them at the door.

I smiled and said, "Come on in out of the rain."

Grace didn't hesitate. She stepped in and Daniel followed. They wiped their feet on the mat and hung their raincoats on the grab rail by the door.

Abby soon joined us, and we moved to the dinette table where Grace and Daniel sat on one side, Abby and I on the other. Daniel spoke first.

"We brought the Jeep. It's ready to go. New battery, new tires, new shocks and a complete tune-up. Even has a full tank of gas.

"But, here's the thing. Grace told me why you wanted to buy it. To go look for your friend up on Crystal Mountain. The Jeep is the right vehicle for that. It will get you there and back. But there's no need for you to buy it."

He reached into his pocket and pulled out a set of keys. "Just take it. Use it for as long as you need and when you're done, bring it back to my shop. We'll write it off as a long test drive. There won't be any charge, and you won't have to buy something you don't really need."

He held out the keys, waiting for Abby to take them.

She looked into his eyes for a moment then reached over and closed her hand around his. "Daniel, I appreciate the offer. But I'm buying the Jeep. I've been looking for one like it for a while, and I don't want to let it slip away. So, I'm buying it. If you've got the title, I've got the money."

He smiled. "If you're sure you want to buy it, I'll sell it to you. But we don't have to do it tonight. You can drive it for a few days. If you change your mind, it won't bother me a bit. Just bring it back, and we'll be square."

Abby smiled again. "Daniel, you're a good man, and I appreciate what you're trying to do, but my mind is made up. I want to buy the Jeep."

She took the keys from him and reached into her back pocket and pulled out a stack of hundred-dollar bills. A small portion of what she had won at the casino.

She put the money on the table and slid it over to him. "Thirty-five hundred dollars. I think that covers it."

He looked at the money but didn't touch it. Instead, he said, "I can take a check if you don't want to part with all that cash."

She shook her head. "I didn't bring my checkbook, so cash works for me. You have the title?"

Daniel looked over at Grace. "She does."

Grace reached inside her shirt and pulled out a tan envelope with an Arkansas title, a bill of sale, and an odometer statement.

She handed the papers to Abby. "It's an open title. Daniel has already signed it and the bill of sale. All you have to do is write in the price and put your name on it, and it'll be legal.

"We put a temp tag on it so you won't get stopped. It'll be good for another ten days. After that, you'll need to get it registered."

Abby nodded. "So, it's outside, right? Can I go out and sit in it?"

Daniel and Grace answered at the same time. "Yes, it's outside. And it's yours. You can do whatever you want in it."

Abby started to get up, but I stopped her. I had a question for Daniel. "How much to put a tow bar and lights on it so we can haul it behind the motorhome?"

He smiled. "I figured you might want to do that. It's already got a got a base plate and is wired for towing, so all you need is the tow bar. I can get one and put it on for just under three hundred."

Abby counted out three one hundred-dollar bills and slid them over. "Call me when you're ready to put it on."

He nodded. "Will do. Plan on day after tomorrow."

He stood and reached out to shake her hand. "Pleasure doing business with you. Now let's go out and I'll show you how everything works."

It was still raining, but just barely. Daniel and Grace grabbed their raincoats but didn't bother to put them on. I opened the door and we all went out to look at Abby's new 1999 Jeep Cherokee.

Chapter Twenty-Nine

The sun had set an hour earlier, and in the darkness of the RV park the two Cherokees were almost hidden.

From a distance, all that could be seen was the reflection of their headlights. Daniel produced a flashlight and lit up the one Abby had bought. With raindrops puddled on the hood, the green paint glistened. It looked almost new.

Abby walked over and opened the driver's door. The overhead light came on, illuminating the interior as well as the smile on her face. She sat in the driver's seat and put both hands on the wheel. Daniel opened the passenger door and slid in beside her. Grace and I stood a few feet away and listened as Daniel explained the controls and answered Abby's questions.

After a few minutes of watching, Grace turned to me and asked, "You really going up to Crystal Mountain?"

I nodded. "Yeah, we are."

She looked up at the still cloudy sky and said, "You're not going tonight, are you?"

I nodded again. "Yeah, probably."

She shook her head. "I wouldn't go up there at night, especially after a rain. Not unless someone I cared for was up there and needed help."

I didn't know whether Kat was up there or not and, if she was, whether she needed our help. But I didn't want to risk not going.

Grace could tell I had made up my mind about the trip and she said, "I guess there's no way I can talk you out of it."

I shrugged. "No, there's not."

"That's what I thought. So, if you go up there, you have to promise you'll be careful. Go slow and stay out of the ditches. Take blankets, boots and a charged-up cell phone. There probably won't be cell service, but if you run into trouble and have a signal, call me.

"Even if you don't run into trouble, call me no later than eight tomorrow morning and let me know you made it back. If you don't call, I'll figure you're stuck in the mud, and I'll come looking for you."

I shook my head. "Grace, I can't call you. I don't have your number."

She pulled out her phone and handed it to me. "Call your phone on mine."

I punched in the number and held the phone until I heard mine ringing inside the motorhome. Then I ended the call and handed the phone back to Grace.

"Done. Your number is on my phone. I'll call or text you when we get back. If you don't hear from me before eight in the morning, call me before you go out looking for us."

She nodded. "Will do."

We turned our attention back to Daniel and Abby. They seemed to be finishing up inside the Jeep. Abby had started the motor and had tested the headlights, signals and wipers. Everything seemed to work.

Satisfied with her purchase, she killed the motor and walked over to where Grace and I were standing. She said, "It's exactly what I've been looking for, a little Jeep wagon in good condition with air conditioning. I even like the green color."

Daniel walked over to join us and as soon as he got close, Abby gave him a hug. "Thanks for selling me the Jeep. I'm going to keep it for a long time."

She turned to Grace and said, "Your brother is a good man. If he ever needs anything, let me know."

After saying their goodbyes, Daniel and Grace got in the other green Jeep and headed back to their shop. As soon as they were out of sight, Abby went over and patted the hood of her new Jeep and said, "You ready to head up the mountain?"

I wasn't sure where she was talking to me or the Jeep. Neither one of us answered.

Chapter Thirty

Not hearing an answer to her question, Abby asked again, this time while looking at me. "Walker, you ready to head up the mountain?"

I was pretty sure she already knew the answer. Her mind was made up and she was only asking to make me feel like I was included in the decision. At least that's what I thought.

Instead of answering, "Yes," I said, "I think we should go. We don't know if Kat is up there or not, but we have to check. It'd be bad if she was stuck and we didn't do anything. It's not like we have anything else to do tonight."

Abby smiled. "That was what I was hoping you'd say because, even if you didn't want to go, I was going. By myself, if I had to."

A clap of thunder in the distance announced the approach of a second storm. If we were going to go, we needed to leave soon before the heavy rain turned the dirt roads into slop, if it hadn't already done so.

I motioned to the motorhome. "Let's go inside and get ready."

Abby led the way, and I followed. Inside, we gathered up a few supplies. A blanket, a first aid kit, a six pack of water, three large trash bags to use as makeshift raincoats, and the map we'd gotten from Digger. We weren't expedition ready, but we had most of the basics. The only thing missing was food.

We hadn't eaten since earlier in the day, and my stomach was rumbling. It was saying, "Fooooood." It knew we needed to eat, especially if we were heading out into the wild with a good chance of getting stuck and having to spend the night in the Jeep. I didn't want to have to do that on an empty stomach.

I turned to Abby, "You hungry?"

She nodded. "Yeah, starting to get that way. What do you have in mind?"

"Burgers. From Burger King. There's one about five miles back, across from the Hot Springs Village gate. We could get food there. Wouldn't take long."

She nodded. "Sounds good to me. You ready to go?"

"Almost. All I need to do is top off Bob's food and lock up in here."

She motioned to the door. "You do that, and I'll put our supplies in the Jeep."

She went outside and I went back to top off Bob's food and water bowls. I let him know we'd be away for a bit, but he didn't seem to care. He was in one of his "if you love me, let me sleep" moods.

I left him to his nap and went through the motorhome lowering the privacy shades. I didn't think anyone would try to break in, but in a campground you never know who your neighbors are. They could be saints or they could be sinners. Having the privacy shades down kept them guessing whether anyone was inside or not.

With the motorhome buttoned up, I grabbed the remaining supplies, locked the doors, and headed outside to join Abby in her new Jeep.

She was sitting in the driver's seat, fiddling with

something on the dash. The back hatch was open, probably because that's where she wanted me to put the supplies I was carrying. I unloaded them, closed the hatch and joined her up front.

As soon as I settled in on the passenger seat, I asked, "You want me to drive?"

She smiled and shook her head. "Walker, I know you're asking just to be polite. It's not that you think I can't drive a stick, right?"

There was only one correct answer to the question, and I knew it. "Yep, I'm asking just to be polite. I totally trust your driving skills."

She nodded. "That's what I thought you'd say. Now buckle up and hold on."

The truth was I'd never seen her drive anything. Not a car, truck or motorhome. I didn't know if she knew how to drive or not or, if she did, whether she could drive a stick. But I was about to find out.

She started the motor, put the Jeep in first gear and we headed out. I was immediately impressed with how well she handled the five-speed transmission. She shifted the gears and worked the clutch like someone who had been doing it all their life. It was obvious it wasn't the first time she'd driven a manual.

When we reached the highway, she turned right, away from Crystal Mountain, toward Burger King. She quickly got the Jeep up to speed and, judging from her smile, I could tell she was enjoying how it drove.

At one point, she took both hands off the wheel and said, "Look at this, steady as it can be."

The Jeep tracked true, not pulling to either side, which was a good sign. Maybe it was in better condition than the two hundred thousand miles on the odometer suggested.

We quickly reached Burger King, and Abby pulled up to the speaker at the drive thru. She ordered two Whopper Juniors, two small fries, an apple pie, and two large Mellow Yellows. She didn't bother to ask what I wanted; she just placed her order and drove up to the window to pay.

She paid for the food, handed me the bag and pulled back out on the highway, this time going north toward the dirt road that would lead us to Crystal Mountain.

After getting the Jeep up to speed, she asked me to unwrap a burger for her and set one of the bags of fries in her lap. We were going to eat on the run. I unwrapped the burger, put the fries where she wanted them, and she ate while she drove.

Following her lead, I ate one of the burgers and most of the remaining fries and washed it down with the Mellow Yellow. It probably wasn't the healthiest combination of food, but it was better than riding on an empty stomach.

It didn't take us long to get to FR 132, the Forest Service Road that supposedly led to Crystal Mountain. Abby slowed and pulled onto the road and stopped.

She turned to me and asked, "You have the map?"

I did.

"Good, you read the directions and I'll follow."

I nodded. "Okay. First thing, set your trip odometer to zero."

She looked at the dash and pressed the button that said 'Trip Reset' until it showed zero.

 "Now what?"

"Go down this dirt road for three-point-seven miles. That's where we go left. Then, at four-point-eight miles, we go to the right."

She looked down at the shift lever and moved the transfer case into four-wheel drive. She put the Jeep into first, and we headed slowly down the road.

The Jeep's headlamps did a pretty good job of lighting up the path directly in front of us but didn't penetrate the dark forest on either side. A layer of water on the road, a couple of inches deep, glistened with the reflection of our lights.

Deep ruts suggested another vehicle had traveled the road recently. I couldn't tell if they were going up the mountain or heading back to the highway, but if the driver had any sense, they'd be heading toward pavement, away from the dirt road we were on.

At the three-point-five-mile mark, Abby said, "We're almost to the first turn. Tell me when you see it."

The windshield was starting to fog up from all the humidity and Abby had the defroster on full trying to keep the glass clear. The rain had returned; small random drops at first, then a steady downpour. Lightning in the distance gave us a snapshot of the surrounding mountains.

We'd gone less than four miles since leaving pavement, but it felt like we had traveled into a distant world—one without artificial lights or signs of human habitation.

At exactly three-point-seven miles, the road veered to the left, just like the map had said it would. I pointed and said, "There, to the left, go that way."

Abby nodded, shifted down from third into second, and kept the Jeep going the right direction. The tracks we had been following, the ones that had left the deep ruts, were no longer with us. The steady rain on the dirt road had melted them away.

The whine of the Jeep's four-wheel drive transmission was

reassuring. It created a sense of invincibility. If anything could conquer this road, it would be the Jeep. At least that's what I hoped.

At the four-point-three mark, Abby slowed and asked, "Where's the turn? There's supposed to be one here."

I rechecked Digger's map and quickly saw the problem. "The turn is at four-point-eight, about a half mile ahead of us."

Abby nodded, downshifted into first and drove on. The trip odometer had just clicked over to four-point-six when she suddenly slowed. She pointed out the window and said, "Somebody's on the road, up ahead."

I wiped the fog from my side to get a better view. She was right; someone was standing in the road ahead of us. Waving a flashlight, trying to get our attention.

Chapter Thirty-One

"What are you folks doing out here this time of night?"

The man asking, the one who had been holding the flashlight and standing in the middle of the road, was wearing a Forest Service poncho with a badge clipped on the front.

He had walked up to Abby's side of the Jeep and signaled her to roll down the window. It was raining, and she rolled it down just enough to talk.

While she was doing this, the ranger swept his flashlight through the Jeep, checking the back seats, and then checking me.

He repeated his question. "What are you folks doing out here this rainy night?"

This time, Abby answered. "We're looking for a friend. We think she drove her rental car up on the mountain. She hasn't returned, so we came out looking for her."

The ranger nodded. "Your friend? What kind of car was she driving?"

"A rental. A Kia, I think."

The Ranger nodded again. "You folks part of the Rainbow camp?"

Abby shook her head. "No, we're not with them. We're staying over at Coleman's, trying to find our friend. Have you seen her?"

The ranger, standing the rain, pointed down the road and said, "I don't know if it is your friend's or not, but there's a car on the side of the road up near where people park to dig crystals. When I checked on it, no one was inside.

"I don't recommend going up there. The road is pretty messy and with this rain it'll get worse. Be better if you just went back and waited for daylight. There's a turn-around just ahead."

He focused his flashlight toward a wide spot in road just in front of us. "Right up there. See it? It's a good place to turn around."

Abby nodded, thanked the ranger and rolled up her window. He stepped back, and she put the Jeep in gear and headed where he had pointed. When we reached the turn around, she kept going. She wasn't about to go back and wait till morning.

With both hands on the wheel and her eyes on the road, she asked, "We still going the right way?"

I looked at the map. "Yep. According to this we are. We veer right in point two miles. Then we go straight until the odometer shows fourteen. That'll put us at the Crystal Mountain parking area."

Abby nodded and kept driving, keeping both hands on the wheel except when she needed to shift gears. The little Jeep hadn't missed a beat, but as the road conditions got worse it was taking more work to keep it on track. The combination of the muddy surface and the hidden rocks underneath made for a rough and challenging drive.

At four-point-eight miles, she saw the turnoff to the right and took it. The road was narrower than the one we had been on and immediately went up a steep hill. Small streams of mud cascaded down it, exposing rocks and the occasional glint of crystals.

Abby had downshifted into second to make the climb; the little Jeep responded with a surge of power. It was built for these kinds of challenges.

When the road leveled out, she shifted into third and asked, "You think it's her car? The one the ranger said was parked up there?"

I didn't know the answer and I couldn't figure out why there wasn't anyone in it. With the rain and dropping temps, being inside the car would be the safest place. Even if it were stuck in the mud, it would provide dry shelter. Kat would know that and would be inside unless she was unable to get to it.

I didn't mention this to Abby. All I said was, "I hope it's her car and I hope she's in it."

I expected Abby to have more to say about it. But she didn't. She just drove, in silence. With the rain beating down even harder, it was getting difficult to carry on a conversation in the Jeep. Maybe that's why she wasn't talking. Or maybe her 'gift' was giving her bad news.

At the five-point-three mark, we went uphill again for another long stretch. At the seven-point-one mark, the road flattened out for a mile then headed up again. The uphill runs were the hardest. Abby would downshift and the Jeep would surge at first but then slow as the steady climb against gravity took its toll.

When we reached a flat section, she'd shift into a higher gear and gain a bit of speed. But with the added speed, she had to be careful. The rain had turned the loose dirt on the top of the road into a slippery muck. Too much traction would spin the tires, and the Jeep would slide toward the ditch on one side or the steep drop-off on the other.

The hidden rocks were another problem. When the Jeep's front tires hit a big one, the steering wheel would push away from the rock, taking us in an unexpected direction. With the narrow road, the rain, the slick mud and the hidden rocks, Abby was working hard to keep the Jeep from going over the edge.

I could tell she was getting tired. The see-saw action of the wheel, the constant shifting gears, the pushing of the clutch and the stress of being out on a dark dirt road in a rainstorm in the middle of the night were taking a toll on her.

I was tempted to volunteer to take the wheel, but seeing the determined look on her face, I decided if she wanted me to drive, she'd let me know. So I kept my eyes on the road ahead, the odometer and the map.

Forty minutes after leaving pavement, we had covered thirteen miles. As the navigator, I let Abby know. "We're almost there. Just another mile."

She nodded but said nothing. She just kept driving.

Just before the odometer reached fourteen, we saw a car on the side of the road ahead of us. A Kia with its back tires sunk deep in the mud. We had finally found what we had been looking for.

Abby dropped the Jeep into first and rolled up behind the car, close enough so the Jeep's headlights lit up the interior. She shifted into neutral, set the parking brake, and looked over at me.

"You want to get out and see if anyone is in it?"

It struck me as funny the way she said, "if anyone is in it." Instead of saying Kat's name, she said "anyone," like she already knew Kat wouldn't be inside.

We'd left the motorhome in such a rush that I'd forgotten

to bring the rubber boots we'd bought at Walmart. They would have come in handy walking in the muck just outside my door.

Still, we had gotten this far and found what I hoped was Kat's car, so I wasn't going to be too worried about getting mud on my tennis shoes. I opened the passenger door, hopped out and immediately sank to my ankles in the mud. It was soft and cooler than I expected.

The rain was still coming down and I was getting wet, so I didn't waste any time getting over to the car. I pulled out the flashlight I'd brought with me and swept the interior. There was no one inside, but there were signs someone had been digging crystals.

A wicker basket in the back seat was filled with them. Next to it, a dirt encrusted screwdriver, the kind sold back at the mine. Next to the screwdriver an empty water bottle.

There was a stack of newspapers in the front passenger seat, next to another basket filled with crystals, some wrapped in paper. A brochure for Hot Springs Village, the retirement center we'd passed on the way to our campsite, sat on the dash. A pair of lady's sandals lay on the floor under the steering wheel.

I checked the doors and all were locked, which meant I couldn't get inside, but it was clear no one was in the car. I went back to the Jeep and climbed into the front beside Abby, my shoes dripping mud on her clean floor mats. She didn't seem to mind, or if she did, she didn't say anything.

I reported my findings. "No one in the car. Doors locked. Baskets of crystals on the seats. Lady's sandals on the floor. Empty water bottle in the back. No sign of a struggle."

Abby nodded but said nothing. After a moment I asked, "So what do you think?"

I figured she could use her 'gift' to sense things out. If she couldn't, maybe she'd think of something I'd missed.

Instead of answering my question, she said, "Watch your feet. You're getting mud in my new Jeep. I've only had it an hour, and you're already getting it dirty."

I laughed because if she thought the inside was getting dirty, she should see the outside. From the windows down, the green Jeep was now mostly brown from the mud being thrown up by the tires.

We were still parked behind the empty car trying to figure out what to do next when Abby started working the horn, one long beep followed by several short beeps.

The Jeep's horn was loud. Not the polite, "Please excuse me" sound of newer cars. In the Jeep, it was more like, "Get the heck out of my way, you moron!"

It was loud enough to be heard for miles. If anyone was nearby, they would hear it. Abby was using it as a beacon, letting whoever had left the car, know we were there.

A minute after the first set of horn blasts, she repeated the sequence. One long blast followed by several short ones.

Then we waited.

Chapter Thirty-Two

With the windows in the Jeep rolled up to keep the rain out, they had fogged almost as soon as we'd stopped. With the two of us inside and the high humidity outside, fogging was inevitable.

Every few minutes, we'd use our shirt sleeves to wipe the fog away so we could see. Abby would blast the horn; we'd wait a minute or two and then wipe the windows to see if anyone had responded.

After fifteen minutes, no one had.

It was dark up on Crystal Mountain. There were no streetlights, and the stars and moon were hidden by the thick clouds of the rainstorm. Anyone in the woods without a flashlight could easily get lost. On a rainy night, trying to find your way off the mountain, cold and wet without a light, would be a struggle.

The Jeep's headlights were on and could be seen maybe a hundred feet down the road. But in the woods off to the side, they wouldn't be noticed. Thinking about this, I turned to Abby and said, "Use the flashers."

The Jeep, like most modern cars, had bright yellow emergency lights that would flash on and off. The flashing was designed to attract maximum attention, letting nearby drivers see and avoid a stalled or broken-down vehicle.

Up on Crystal Mountain, the flashing lights might help guide someone in the woods back to the safety of the road.

Abby looked over at me and said, "Cover your ears."

I knew what she was going to do and put my hands over my ears. Again.

She grinned and hit the horn. This time, a succession of blasts, lasting a minute, spaced about five seconds apart.

With my hands occupied trying to keep from going deaf, I wasn't able to clear the fog off the windshield and almost missed seeing a faint flicker of light in the woods. It was off to our left and I wasn't really sure if I'd seen the light or not. It could have been lightning in the distance or a strange reflection off the Jeep's headlights.

I leaned into the windshield and wiped a circle with my sleeve. Looking out, I saw the light again. A faint beam moving through the woods.

I pointed to it and said, "Abby, you see that? There's someone out there."

Not waiting for an answer, I opened the door and went back out in the rain and mud, heading toward the light. Someone was coming down Crystal Mountain, flashlight in hand and I wanted to see who it was.

I turned back to Abby, who was still inside the Jeep and yelled, "Honk the horn."

I only had to say it once. She laid on the horn and, with me standing just in front of it, I learned firsthand how loud it actually was. Way more than would be legal in most civilized countries.

Instinctively, I covered my ears, blocking out some of the noise. I turned back to face Abby and shook my head, hoping she understood I wanted her to get off the horn.

Thankfully, she got the message.

I turned back to where I had seen the light and, just as I

did, I saw someone stumble out of the woods onto the road.

I couldn't tell if it was Kat or not. The height was right, but without getting closer I wouldn't know for sure; I went over to check.

As I got close, I could see it was a woman. Wet from head to toe. Shivering. Unable to speak. But it wasn't Kat.

I ran up to her and said, "We're here to help. The Jeep over there, it's dry and warm inside. Follow me."

The woman hesitated, seeing a stranger on the cold wet mountain wasn't what she expected. But she was cold and tired, and the warmth of the Jeep sounded better than standing in the rain.

I ran to it, and she followed. When we got there, she again hesitated. She wasn't sure she wanted to get into the Jeep with a strange man. I opened the driver's side passenger door and pointed to the seat. The woman shook her head and looked at her own car. She was trying to decide which would be safest.

Abby saw her indecision and called out to her. "Get in and get dry."

The woman, hearing Abby's voice, took a seat and I closed the door behind her. I ran to the other side of the Jeep, intending to get in the back seat next to her. But Abby stepped out and stopped me. She said, "Might be better if I did it."

She was probably right. Our guest might feel more comfortable with a woman sitting beside her than a man, so Abby got in the back and I took her place up front. I watched as she wrapped the woman in a blanket and held her hand while telling her everything was going to be all right.

The woman, who had been crying when I found her,

tried to speak but was unable to. She could only grunt. Looking around, she saw the bottles of water and pointed at one and then at her mouth. It was easy to figure out what she wanted.

Abby grabbed a bottle and handed it to her. The woman took it without hesitation, twisted off the top and took a long drink. She closed her eyes, leaned her head back and shook some of the rain water from her hair.

She took another sip and after a moment spoke the first words she said since we'd found her. She said, "Ccccooooldd."

Abby turned to me and said, "Put the heater on high. Let's warm it up in here."

The Jeep's motor had been running since we stopped, and it didn't take long for it to start blowing warm air. As soon as the woman in the back felt the heat flowing from the front vents, she smiled and nodded.

A few minutes later, she spread her arms, loosening the blanket that had been wrapped around her. She took another sip of water and asked, "Whaaaaat time is it?"

Abby, who wasn't wearing a watch, answered. "After nine."

The woman shook her head and said, "I need to call my husband. He'll be worried."

I pulled out my phone and looked at the display. Abby had been right. It was after nine. But we weren't going to be making any calls. The phone showed zero bars.

I showed it to her and she nodded. She asked the woman, "Are you out here alone? Anyone else with you?"

"No. Just me. No one else."

She looked over and saw the Burger King bag. Abby noticed and said, "We have apple pie. Would you like it?"

The woman nodded.

Abby handed her the pie along with the plastic fork it came with. But the woman didn't use the fork; she pulled the pie out of the little box and gobbled it down. When she was done, she wiped the crumbs and apple juice from around her mouth and said, "Thank you—for the food, the water and for finding me. I was lost up there, I couldn't find my way back to the road."

She reached for the door. She wanted to get out but couldn't figure out how to open it.

Abby stopped her. "You don't want to go out there. Stay in here, where it's warm."

The woman shook her head. "I can't stay. I've got to go back. My husband will be worried."

"Your husband? Is he up on the mountain? Is that why you need to go back?"

She shook her head. "No, he's not up there. He's at our condo in the Village. He'll be worried I haven't called or returned."

Abby nodded. "I understand. But your car is stuck in the mud, and it's not going anywhere. We'll take you back to your husband if you want us to."

The woman looked out the window at her car and asked, "Will it be okay to leave it here?"

Abby nodded. "Yeah, it'll be okay. But if there is anything in it you're worried about, we can it take it with us."

The woman smiled and in a weak voice said, "I know this sounds silly, but I worked too hard finding those crystals to leave them here. I need to take them with me."

She reached for the door, but again Abby stopped her. "You don't need to go out in the rain. He'll get the crystals

199

for you."

She tapped me on the shoulder and said, "Go."

I was already wet and muddy and getting back out in the rain to get the crystals wasn't going to change anything. I took a deep breath, pushed the door open and trudged through ankle deep mud to get to the passenger side of the woman's car. Just as I reached it, the car's headlights flashed and the doors unlocked. Looking back toward the Jeep, I could see the woman holding up the car's remote. She'd unlocked the doors for me.

I opened the front and grabbed the basket of crystals, the ones that had been carefully wrapped in newspaper. I figured these were the ones she wanted. I carried the basket back to the Jeep, opened the front passenger door, and put it on the seat.

I went back to the car, grabbed the basket from the rear seat, brought it back to the Jeep and put it in on the front passenger side floorboard. Then I went to the driver's side of the Jeep, shook off as much wet as I could and took a seat behind the wheel. Abby wouldn't be happy with the thick globs of wet mud I'd tracked in; but she could worry about that later.

As soon as I got in, she tapped me on the shoulder and said, "Walker, I want you to meet Haley."

I turned and smiled, and said, "Good to meet you. Looks like you had some luck digging crystals."

Her eyes lit up. "It's amazing up there. Everywhere you look, there's crystals. Nice ones. I started finding phantoms and double terminated points, and I couldn't stop."

Abby tapped me on the shoulder. "Think you can get us back to the highway without wrecking?"

I was pretty sure I could. The hardest part would be

finding a place to turn around on the narrow dirt road. But the Jeep was fairly small and it wouldn't need much space.

Since I was already sitting in the driver's seat, I put the Jeep in first and pulled around Haley's car. There was a wide spot in front of it where others had parked and I used it to get the Jeep turned around.

As we passed back by Haley's car, she said, "I don't feel right leaving it here. It's a rental. If anything happens to it, I'll have to pay extra."

Abby said, "Don't worry about it. Your car will be fine. You can come back and get it in the morning. Right now, we need to get you off the mountain so you can call your husband."

Haley understood. Her car could wait.

I drove slowly, trying to follow the tracks we'd made when we came in. Rain had filled most of them, but the mud hadn't gotten much deeper. It looked like the dirt road had been built on a solid rock base. Our tires plowed through the mud and gained traction on the hard surface below.

As I drove, I could hear Haley in the back seat explaining how she and her husband had won a timeshare vacation at Hot Springs Village. They had come up from Mississippi to check the place out. After sitting through the mandatory sales pitch, she decided she wanted to go to the nearby mine to dig crystals. Her husband volunteered to go with her, but she knew he'd rather stay in the condo and watch TV, so she went alone.

She took their rental car to the mine where she met a man who told her about Crystal Mountain and the Crystal Cave. He showed her some crystals and said she could find ones like his up there. The man's crystals were so nice and his story so intriguing, she paid him twenty dollars for a map showing how to get to Crystal Mountain.

She had followed the directions, had parked where he said to park and had found crystals where he said they'd be. But she hadn't found the Crystal Cave.

When she paused, Abby asked her, "Did you see anyone else up there?"

Haley thought for a moment then said, "I did. Another woman. She was there when I got there. She showed me some of the crystals she had and told me where she had found them. She was real nice but didn't stay long. I heard a car leave about twenty minutes after I saw her. I think it was hers."

Abby nodded. "Did she say where she was staying or where she was going next?"

Haley shook her head. "We talked about crystals, not much else. She did say something about another mine. I think she called it the Surrender Mine. I don't know if she'd already been there or was going there next. I was so excited about the crystals I was finding that I really didn't pay much attention to what she was saying."

Abby nodded. "What did she look like?"

Haley squinted, "She was big. Probably six foot tall. Frizzy, red hair. Wearing overalls. You'd remember her if you saw her. She a friend of yours?"

Abby shook her head. "No. The one we're looking for is not that tall. Just barely over five foot. Dark hair, cut short. You didn't see her up on the mountain?"

Haley shook her head. "No, I didn't see her. Just the tall redhead."

Abby said nothing for a moment then asked, "What about the guy?"

Haley cocked her head. "What guy?"

"Wasn't there a guy up there? After the woman left?"

She thought for a moment then said, "You're right! There was a guy. But he wasn't digging crystals. He was looking for a cat. It was the strangest thing.

"I was coming down the mountain to load some crystals into my car, and there was this guy. He was standing by my car window, looking in."

"I asked him what he was doing, and he said he was looking for a cat. I didn't know why he thought there'd be a cat in my car, but there wasn't one, and I told him so.

"He didn't look dangerous or anything, but you never know these days. I told him my husband was right behind me and wouldn't like the idea of a stranger messing with our car.

"He apologized and left. But it was strange; he kept calling out for his cat. He kept yelling, "Cat," over and over, like he expected his cat to hear him and come running."

Abby nodded. "This guy, what was he driving?"

Haley shook her head. "He wasn't driving anything as far as I could tell. He was walking. I figured he was part of the Rainbow crowd. Their camp is on the other side of the mountain.

"He looked like he could have been one of them. Long hair, unshaven, dirty clothes. Up here on the mountain on foot. I almost felt sorry for him. And his cat.

"I probably should have loaded up my car right then and left. That would have been the smart thing to do. I'd already found a lot of nice crystals and I was getting tired. It looked like rain so I should have left right then.

"But I didn't. Instead of leaving, I went back up the

mountain. I couldn't help myself. The crystals up there are so nice. I was still finding them when the rain came. When it got heavy, I came down to my car and tried to leave. But it got stuck. The tires just spun in the mud.

"Instead of doing the smart thing and staying in the car, I went back up the mountain to get more crystals."

She put her hands on her rain flattened hair and sighed. "I should have left before the rain started."

She was right. She should have got off the mountain before the rain started. But if she had, we wouldn't have found her, or learned about the redheaded woman or the guy looking for his cat.

By the time we reached the highway, the rain had let up and we had a cell signal. Haley called her husband and let him know she was okay and he was relieved to hear her voice. He said he'd be waiting for us at the Hot Springs Village gate.

True to his word, he was there when we arrived. In a golf cart he had borrowed from a timeshare neighbor. The cart was his only other form of transportation because their rental car was back on Crystal Mountain stuck in the mud.

But he didn't seem to care about the car. He knew it could be replaced, but not his wife, who he seemed to truly love. He stood by her side and held her hand as she told him how we had found her. He thanked us profusely and offered us money for our trouble. Of course, we didn't take any.

We were happy to have helped his wife and to have learned what had happened up on the mountain that day. The husband gave us his business card and said to call him if we ever needed anything. They piled into the golf cart and started to ride off, but then did a U-turn and headed back toward us. Haley hopped out and said, "Almost forgot my crystals! I can't leave them."

She walked over to the Jeep and pointed at the baskets in the front seat. "Those are my babies."

Abby opened the door and I grabbed one of the baskets and Haley grabbed the other. I took mine to the golf cart, but Haley took hers to the hood of the Jeep and motioned Abby to come over and see what she'd found.

She picked up one of the crystals wrapped in newspaper and carefully peeled the paper away revealing a perfectly clear double terminated quartz crystal about eight inches long It had natural symmetrical facets with sharp points on both ends. It looked too perfect to be real, but it was real. Haley had found it on the mountain.

She handed it to Abby. "This is for you for coming to my rescue."

Abby reached out and touched the crystal, but she didn't take it from Haley. Instead, she shook her head and said, "No, you keep it. It's already brought you good luck. It'll bring you more."

Haley smiled and closed her hand around the gem. She took a deep breath, opened her hand and said, "Please. Take it. It's telling me it belongs with you."

Abby nodded as if she understood what Haley was saying. She smiled, reached out and ever so gently took the crystal from her. She held it tightly with both hands, which brought a smile to Haley's face. Without words, the two women had used the crystal to pass a message between them.

Whatever message the crystal had sent, had made both of them happy.

Haley picked up her basket and walked over to her husband who had been watching the two women from his seat in the golf cart. He didn't question what had just transpired. He seemed to understand.

She sat down beside him, holding her basket of crystals in her lap. They waved at us and drove off.

Abby looked at me and said, "That will be us some day, sitting side by side in a golf cart, driving away in the sunset."

I could have broken the mood by saying the sun had set six hours earlier and that there was little chance that Abby and I would ever be in a golf cart together. But I was tired, my feet were wet, my pants covered in mud. All I wanted to do was get back to the motorhome, dry off and get some sleep.

Chapter Thirty-Three

Bob was waiting for us when we got back to the RV. Abby went in first and he was all over her. He rubbed up against her ankles and cried like a baby. When she bent down to pet him, I tried to step around her, but she stopped me.

She put her finger on my chest and said, "Before you come in here, you need to pull off your wet clothes. Everything down to your undies. I don't want you tracking mud in here."

I was too tired to argue, so I sat down on the entry steps and pulled off my muddy socks and shoes. I stood and stripped off my shirt and dropped my pants. Abby nodded her approval and said, "Okay cowboy, you can come in now. But you need to take a quick shower and clean up. No way you're getting into bed with me like that."

I was halfway back to the bathroom before I realized what she had said, something about getting in bed with her. That was the last thing on my mind, getting in bed with Abby. All I wanted to do was get warm, get clean, and get some sleep.

It had been a long day that had started out in the casino parking lot in Vicksburg, followed by a two-hundred-fifty mile drive to the crystal mine, then two hours talking to Digger, followed by a rough ride up Crystal Mountain road. I had gotten out into the wet rain, waded in ankle deep mud, and rescued a woman who was lost and not Kat.

After all that, I was bone tired and bothered by the fact that we hadn't found who we were looking for.

I took a quick shower, pulled on a T-shirt and clean shorts and came out to find Abby sitting on the couch, a half empty glass of wine in hand.

She looked up and smiled. "Feel better?"

I nodded. "Yeah, I do. Now I need to get some sleep. It's been a long day."

I headed to the back bedroom, to the bed Abby had slept in the night before. My plan was to get there before she did, get in the bed and lock the door behind me. She could sleep on the couch like I had done on the previous night.

My plan would have worked, except that when I got to the bedroom, the door was locked. Somehow, Abby had gotten there before me, locked the door from the outside and taken her place on the couch.

Like most motorhomes, the bedroom door in mine was made of flimsy hollow core wood. I could have hit it with my shoulder and busted it open. But if I had, it'd be me who'd have to fix it and it would be more trouble than it was worth. I went back up front to ask Abby why the door was locked.

She was still sitting on the couch, wine glass now empty, waiting for me. She pointed to the box of Chardonnay on the counter, held out her glass and said, "Top me off, will you?"

I saw no reason not to. I brought the box over and filled her glass. I took the wine back to the counter and turned to see what else she wanted me to do. It didn't take long to find out.

She patted the space on the couch beside her and said, "Come over here and sit. We need to talk."

I should have said, "No, I don't need to talk. What I need to do is go to bed." But, instead, I didn't say anything. I just slouched over to the couch and sat down beside her.

She put her arm around my shoulder and said, "I know it's been a long day. I know you must be tired. But it's not over yet. We need to go next door to Kat's motorhome and take care of something. After that, you can come back here and get some sleep."

I nodded. At that point, I would have done anything if it ended with me getting sleep.

She finished her wine, set the glass on the side table, and stood. She pointed at my feet and said, "I found a dry pair of shoes in your closet. Put them on, and we'll go."

She went to the door and waited while I put on the shoes. They were my backup pair. Well broken in and comfortable. As soon as I had them laced up, she said, "Let's go."

Like a puppy on a leash, I followed.

Kat's motorhome was still parked in the next site over, less than twenty feet away. We covered the distance quickly, being careful to avoid the puddles left by the evening's rain.

When we reached the side door, Abby used her key to unlock it. This was easier than going in through the passenger door like we had done earlier. She went up the steps first, and I followed. Since she hadn't bothered to turn on the inside lights, I reached for the switch, but she stopped me.

"No lights," she whispered. "We don't want anyone to know we're here."

She grabbed my hand and led me back to the bedroom. When we reached the door, she let go and went in. I waited outside, expecting her to get whatever she'd come for. But instead of coming back out, she lay down on the bed and patted the space beside her. "Come in and join me. Close the door behind you."

If I hadn't been so sleepy, I would have done the right thing. I would have headed back to my own bed in my own motorhome. But I was tired and Kat's bed looked as comfortable as my own. It was right there in front of me, so I stepped into the bedroom, closed the door, and lay down beside Abby.

Chapter Thirty-Four

All I wanted to do was sleep. I was finally in a comfortable bed and sleep should have come quickly. But sleep wasn't part of Abby's plans. She wanted to talk.

She said, "Remember when I told you how Devin described you? How she said most of the time you were like Clark Kent, mild mannered and easy going?"

Before I could answer, she continued, "Well, so far, she's been right. You've been a perfect gentleman doing all the right things at the right time. I like that about you.

"But Devin also said that when it came to saving damsels in distress, you could quickly turn into Superman or the Hulk, depending on the situation. She said she saw it herself and it was scary.

"I don't know if she was exaggerating or not, but something's going to happen later tonight, and you might need to turn into Superman, at least for a few minutes.

"I want to see Superman, not the Hulk. And I don't want to see any broken furniture or broken bones. All you'll have to do is give someone a scare. Think you can do that?"

She'd pretty much lost me when she called me a perfect gentleman. I think I dozed off after that. But I was pretty sure I heard her ask if I could do something.

I wasn't sure what it was, but I was pretty sure I could do it. So I said, "Yeah, I can do it. Just wake me whenever you need it done."

I rolled over and closed my eyes.

Sometime later, it could have been five minutes or five hours, she tapped me on the shoulder and whispered, "Someone's trying to break in. Get ready."

Still asleep, I mumbled, "Get ready? For what?"

Before she could answer, I heard the outside door open and listened as someone stepped into the motorhome. Abby pushed me out of bed and whispered, "Go see who it is."

I was still half asleep but coming out of it quickly. I could hear someone shuffling around up front. From the way the motorhome rocked with each step they took, I figured they were pretty big.

I eased the bedroom door open and peeked out, wanting to see who was there and what they were armed with before confronting them. It was dark inside the motorhome and the intruder hadn't yet found the light switch. I couldn't see him, and, hopefully, he couldn't see me.

Thinking the cover of darkness would give me an advantage, I quietly opened the bedroom door and tiptoed over to where I thought the intruder was standing. My plan was to grab him from behind in a bear hug.

It would have worked had Abby not flicked on the lights right before I got to him. When she did, the intruder whirled around, saw me, and, with a practiced motion, brought up her hand and blasted me in the face with what I later learned was twenty percent oleo resin pepper spray.

It had an immediate effect, blinding me and filling my eyes with white-hot pain. I tried to bring my hands up to my face to rub the pain away but was stopped by the intruder, who slapped handcuffs on both of my wrists.

A woman's voice commanded, "Down, on the floor. Now!"

Without resisting, I slumped to my knees, using the heels of my cuffed hands to wipe tears away from my eyes.

Behind me, I heard Abby say, "He's not the one you're looking for."

The woman, who seemed surprised I wasn't alone, asked, "Who are you?"

Abby responded, "I'm Kat's cousin, and that man on the floor in front of you is Walker. We're both friends of hers. What are you doing breaking into her motorhome?"

The woman kneeled in front of me, tipped my chin up to get a better look at my face and said, "Oh crap. You're not Dylan. Looks like I made a mistake. Sorry about that."

She moved her hands from my face to the handcuffs around my wrist and fumbled with the key until she was able to get them unlocked.

When my hands were free, I reached up to rub my eyes, but she stopped me. She said, "Don't rub them. It'll only make it worse. You need to flush with water."

She helped me stand and guided me over to the kitchen sink where she turned on the cold water. She put my right hand where I could feel the running water and said, "Get your head down and let the water wash over your eyes."

She sounded like someone who'd dealt with this before, so I did what she said. I bent over and put my head in the sink and hoped the water cure would work.

While I was doing this, the woman spoke with Abby.

She said, "I'm Deputy Betsy Moretti with the Garland County Sheriff's Department, and we have a warrant for Dylan Lancaster. We've been looking for him for three months. Your friend Kat said he might show up here."

Abby asked the same question I would have had my eyes,

213

nose and throat not been burning with pepper spray. "How do you know Kat?"

The deputy took a seat at the kitchen table and Abby sat across from her.

"Three days ago, we got a call about a car stuck in the mud up on Crystal Mountain. I was working the Rainbow camp and I was the closest deputy, so I went to check it out.

"Turns out your friend had gotten her rental stuck. Using the tow rope I carry in my truck, I pulled her out. When I asked where she was staying, she told me she'd driven up from the Keys in her motorhome. She mentioned she came up with a guy named Dylan. Said he came up to get crystals he could take back to Florida to sell.

"When I asked her to describe the guy, he sounded a lot like the man we'd been looking for. Same unusual name, same height, same hair and eye color. Same cover story about buying crystals in Arkansas and taking them back to Florida.

"When she told me this Dylan guy had walked away from the campground and left his things in her motorhome, I suggested we go look. She was reluctant at first, but when I explained we suspected him of dealing drugs, she agreed.

"I followed her to the motorhome, and she gave me permission to look inside. After making sure no one else was in it, I did a quick search. I found his backpack, and inside it, a plastic bag with about two hundred shady eighties. Oxycontin laced with fentanyl.

"It's very dangerous stuff. Not safe to touch with your bare hands. Doesn't take much to kill you. He had a lot of it, which pretty much confirmed our suspicions that he was a major supplier.

"Problem was, I didn't find the drugs in his possession. He wasn't in the RV, just Kat. And because they were in her

214

motorhome, I could have put them on her. But I didn't think she was involved. She wouldn't have let me search if she had known there were drugs there.

"It was Dylan we wanted. He was the main guy. We didn't care about Kat.

"I called my supervisor and explained what I had found and who I thought the drugs belonged to. He agreed that if we could catch Dylan with the drugs, we could leave Kat out of it.

"But we couldn't let her go until we had Dylan in cuffs. We couldn't let her stay in the motorhome with the drugs. She had to move out.

"We figured Dylan would come back for his drugs. Probably sooner than later. And we didn't want her around when he showed up. It would complicate things.

"I had been working undercover at the Rainbow camp and had an old converted school bus parked there that I'd been staying in. It had a few extra beds and I told Kat she could either stay there with me or in a cell at the county jail. Her choice.

"She chose the bus. I had her grab a change of clothes and she followed me over to the Rainbow camp. It was only then that she realized she'd left her phone in the motorhome. That turned out to be a good thing. She wouldn't be calling anyone, and no one could call her. Including Dylan.

"After I got her set up in the school bus, I took her motorhome keys and had our tech guys put a silent alarm on the side door. If anyone opened it, I'd get an alert.

"You guys tripped it earlier today, but I had Dylan in sight and knew it wasn't him so I didn't respond. But when you tripped it again tonight, I got the alert and I came as fast as could, expecting to find Dylan.

"Instead, I find Walker here trying to sneak up on me."

I was still at the sink, trying to flush the pepper spray out of my eyes. With my head under the faucet, the water had found a path down my neck and onto my T-shirt and pants. For the second time that night, I was wet and miserable.

When I could take no more, I stood up, leaned back and tried to clear my throat. The deputy came over and handed me a box of tissues from the kitchen table. She said, "Blow your nose. It'll help."

I grabbed a tissue and started blowing. Nine sheets later, the river of mucus had finally played out. My entire face hurt, eyes, nose, and mouth, but at least I could finally breathe without coughing.

Turning away from the sink, I opened my eyes to see what the deputy looked like. It took me a minute to focus, but when I did, I saw a tall, big-boned, red-headed woman wearing faded blue overalls. She looked like she'd just stepped off the stage of Hee Haw. Not at all what I expected a deputy to look like.

The red hair and overalls reminded me of the woman Haley had told us about earlier. I grabbed a towel from the kitchen counter and wiped the tears from my face. I cleared my throat and said, "You were up on Crystal Mountain today. Kat wasn't with you. Where is she now?"

Chapter Thirty-Five

The deputy didn't answer my question. Instead, she smiled and said, "I'm real sorry about the pepper spray and the cuffs. But you should know better than to sneak up on a woman from behind in the dark. I wouldn't recommend you do it again."

Before I could respond, she asked, "How did you and your lady friend get in here? You have a key?"

I nodded and pointed at Abby. My throat still hurt, and I wasn't up for talking. I let Abby answer the question.

She hesitated, then said, "Kat's father bought the motorhome and gave it to her as a gift. He had a spare key made and kept it in case she got locked out. When he called and said she was missing, he gave me the key and said, 'Go look for her.'

"I convinced Walker to come with me, and we've been on the road ever since. We got up here earlier today and used the key to get in. Kat wasn't here, so we went looking for her. Met a woman up on Crystal Mountain who told us she saw you there, but not Kat. So, where is she?"

Abby had answered the deputy's question. But, like me, she wanted to know where Kat was.

The deputy smiled. "She's safe. Over near Mount Ida. I took her there to stay after I saw Dylan at the Rainbow camp. He was going around asking if anyone had seen Kat, said he needed to talk to her.

"He had a photo of her on his phone, and after he started showing it around, I figured it wouldn't be safe for her to stay there. Sooner or later someone would recognize her and he'd know she was there. So I took her to Sweet Surrender for safety."

Abby crossed her arms like she didn't believe the deputy. "Kat is there now? At Sweet Surrender? If we go over there, we'll find her?"

The deputy nodded. "Yeah, she's over there. If you go over there, you'll see her. But if you go over there now and drive through the gate before sun up, you're liable to be met by someone with a shotgun. They don't like strangers coming in after dark.

"It'd be best if you waited until morning before you made the trip."

She quickly changed the subject. "Where y'all staying?"

Abby motioned over her shoulder. "Next door. In the motorhome."

The deputy smiled. "That's real convenient. Why don't you two go over there and wait for me while I lock this one up? It won't take long."

Abby didn't argue. She got up and helped me to the door. Then she guided me down the steps and back over to my motorhome. She opened the door, and got me inside.

She led me to the couch and we sat, side by side. She took my hand and asked, "Do you believe her?"

My eyes had been closed most of the time the deputy had been talking. I hadn't been able to see her face or watch her body language as she spoke. I could only hear her voice and didn't catch much of what she'd said. Having my head down in the sink with cold water running into my ears wasn't the best way to listen in on a conversation.

Still, the parts I had heard sounded believable. But I wasn't totally sure, so I said, "I don't know. How about you? Do you believe her?"

Abby had been face-to-face with the deputy and had heard everything she had said. She'd been able to look into her eyes and see her facial expressions as she spoke. She would be in a much better position to tell whether the deputy's story was true or not. Plus, she had the 'gift'. Maybe it worked as truth-o-meter.

But apparently, it didn't, because Abby said, "I get the feeling she's telling the truth, at least some of it, but I'm not sure which parts. We need to find out..."

Our conversation was interrupted by a light tap on the door. The deputy was joining us.

Abby let her in, and the first thing the deputy asked was, "Is there anyone else in here?"

Abby shook her head. "No, just us and the cat."

"A cat, huh? Mind if I check?"

I didn't mind, but before I could answer, Abby said, "I want to see an ID. Something that proves you are who you say you are. It's not that I don't trust you, it's just that those overalls are not part of any official police uniform I've seen."

The woman laughed. "This is my hippie look. It lets me fit in over at the Rainbow camp."

She held up the palms of her hands to show she had nothing in them and said, "I've got my badge in my back pocket. I'm going to reach around and pull it out."

With her right hand, she reached behind her and pulled out a small, black wallet. She flipped it open to show an ID with the Garland County Sheriff's Office. Her photo was on the card and below it, her name, rank and the signature of the local sheriff. The card was embossed and looked official.

Abby looked at it, showed it to me and said, "Looks real."

The deputy said, "Yeah, because it is real."

She put it back in her pocket, looked around the motorhome and said, "We need to get you two out of here. Don't want you hanging around messing things up. The best thing you can do is find some other place to camp, maybe near the mine where Kat's staying.

"They don't have a campground there, but there's one nearby at the Highway 27 Fish Village."

The deputy pointed outside. "I'm guessing the green Jeep parked out there is yours. You could drive it to the mine and leave your motorhome at the Fish camp.

"Right now, you need to leave here. I don't want you around if Dylan shows up. You don't have to drive all the way to the Fish Village; you just need to leave here, now.

"You could go the Walmart parking lot just south of Hot Springs Village. They allow overnight RV parking, and it's just a few miles from here. You could go there, stay till morning, then head over to the Fish Village campground."

The deputy looked at me. "Your eyes cleared up enough that you can drive this thing?"

They still stung a bit, but they'd stopped tearing up and pretty much everything was in focus, so I said, "Yeah, I can drive."

"Good. How soon can you leave?"

I looked around the motorhome and all I needed to do was bring the slide room in and unhook from shore power. It wouldn't take long.

"Ten minutes."

"Good. I'll stay until you're ready."

She looked at Abby. "Which one of you has the key to Kat's motorhome?"

Abby had the keys. All of them. She looked at me to see if I wanted to say anything. I didn't, but she did. "Why do you need to know who has a key?"

The deputy frowned, then said, "Because we don't want anyone getting into to Kat's motorhome until we secure the drugs. Give me your keys and I'll make sure to get them back to Kat when this thing is over."

She held out her hand and waited for the keys.

Abby dug in her pocket and pulled out the key with the Ford logo, the one she'd pulled off the ring and we had used to unlock the passenger side door. Before giving it up, she turned to me and said, "Get your phone. Take a picture of me doing this."

I grabbed my phone, hit the camera icon and snapped three photos. Each one clearly showed Abby holding the key over the deputy's open palm.

I showed her the photos and she reluctantly dropped the key into the deputy's hand.

She looked at it and asked, "This the only key you have?"

I knew it wasn't. I knew Abby still had keys to the side door and the outdoor storage compartments, but I wasn't going to say anything. It was up to her to decide how to answer.

She decided to lie. She said, "That's the only key I have. The one to the front door."

The deputy looked at me. "What about you? You have any keys?"

I shook my head. "No. They didn't give me any keys."

She seemed satisfied with my answer and changed the subject. She pointed at the wall behind the couch and asked, "Do you bring the slide in before you unhook or after?"

She was obviously in a hurry to get us out of the park, and I didn't blame her. She had a major drug dealer in her sights and didn't want us to foul things up.

I stood and pressed the button to bring the slide in. It slowly closed the wall, making the motorhome feel a lot smaller inside. When it jolted to a stop, I released the button and pointed to the door. "I need to unhook from shore power."

The deputy followed me outside and watched as I unhooked the power cable, rolled it up and put it in the utility compartment.

Back inside, Abby put everything away and raised the blinds to make it easier for me to drive in the dark.

I made sure the bathroom door was secure and then sat in the driver's seat and started the motor. The deputy watched while I was doing this, like she was making sure I didn't try anything funny. After the motor was started, she turned to Abby. "You driving the Jeep?"

Abby held up her key ring. "Yep."

"Good. The Walmart parking lot is just over the hill. Follow me, and I'll lead the way."

Chapter Thirty-Six

Sixteen minutes later, having left the crystal mine campground and taken the motorhome on the winding, unlit road to the highway, we pulled into the Walmart parking lot. Exactly one hour after midnight.

Walmart was still open, but there weren't many cars in the lot. There were three RVs parked on the north side near a wooded ravine and it looked like they were in for the night.

Figuring that was where Walmart wanted overnight RV'ers to park, I pulled in near them, leaving plenty of space between my motorhome and the others. I didn't want to invade their privacy and didn't want them invading ours.

Abby pulled her Jeep into the empty parking spot next to mine and got out.

The deputy, who had led us to Walmart in her faded gray GMC Jimmy, pulled up near Abby and rolled down her window. She motioned her to come closer so they could talk. She spoke a few words, handed Abby something and drove off. I wasn't able to get outside fast enough to hear what she had said or see what she had given her.

Bob had come up from the back, making noises about how we'd interrupted his beauty sleep. He meowed several times to show his displeasure then turned and trotted back to the bedroom where he hoped to resume his nap. I was hoping to be doing the same soon.

Abby tapped on the side door, letting me know she was

coming in. I'd explained to her earlier that anytime one of us was outside and wanted in, we needed to tap the door so the person inside could make sure Bob wasn't sleeping in the foot well.

If he was there and the door was suddenly opened, he might panic and run out into the parking lot or, worse, into traffic. Either way, it wouldn't be good. He could get lost, get hit by a car or just disappear into the wild. It was something I didn't want to risk, so we had set up the tap routine.

Abby had been good about sticking to it. She tapped on the door, and I checked for Bob. With him safe in the back, I opened it and she came in. She plopped down on the couch and said, "The deputy said not to go back to the campground. She said, no matter what Kat says, don't let her leave the Surrender mine. Not until they get the Dylan thing settled."

It sounded like good advice to me. But even if it weren't, I was too sleepy to care much about what the deputy said. I just wanted sleep.

The night before, Abby had claimed the bed as her own, leaving me the couch. I preferred the bed but was too tired to try to reclaim it. I grabbed a pillow from the overhead bin, folded out the couch and lay down, hoping to sleep.

A few moments after I closed my eyes, I felt Abby's lips brush my cheek as she kissed me good night. She whispered, "Sleep well."

The next thing I remembered was being woken by the sound of the outside door opening. I looked up just in time to see Abby walking in carrying a bag of food from Burger King. It was daylight outside, meaning I'd slept a few hours. It didn't feel like I'd slept hours; but if it was daylight, I had.

She saw me open my eyes and said, "Morning sunshine.

You hungry?"

I was. I sat up, ran my fingers through my hair and nodded. "You went out? I didn't hear you leave."

She smiled. "I tried my best not to wake you. It looked like you needed sleep, so I let you be. I figured that when you woke, you'd be hungry, so I went to Burger King and got us breakfast. Hope you like their sausage and egg croissants."

She put the food on the kitchen table, got a carton of orange juice from the fridge and poured two glasses.

I was still sitting on the couch, trying to wake up, when she came over and rubbed my head. She said, "Come on. It's time to get up. We've got a lot of things to do today, and we need to get on the road.

"I called Kat's father and filled him in on what we learned. He said to call him as soon as we talk to his daughter. I also called Grace and let her know we made it back from Crystal Mountain. She was worried about us going up there and was happy to hear we made it back.

"I didn't tell her about the deputy or about us spending the night in at Walmart. But I did tell her we were moving over to the Fish Village campground. I didn't want her to go back to our old site at the crystal mine looking for us and possibly running into Dylan."

She pointed at the food on the table. "Get up. Come eat with me."

I sighed and pointed to the bathroom. "I'll be right back."

I headed to the back and took care of morning business. I combed my hair, washed my hands and splashed water on my face. On my way back up front, I peeked into the bedroom and saw that Abby had made up the bed and Bob had found his favorite spot in the middle of it, lying in the warmth of a sunbeam.

As I walked by, he looked up and mouthed a soft meow. Then he closed his eyes and went back to sleep. Lucky him.

Up front, Abby had finished her croissant and was cleaning her side of the table. When she was done, she stood and said, "I called the campground, and they had a site available. I went ahead and reserved it.

"The lady said the best way to get there would be to go north on 7 and turn west on 298. She said we'll miss all the Hot Springs traffic going that way."

While Abby was telling me this, I sat down at the table, unwrapped the croissant and took a bite. It was still warm and tasty. Being hungry, it didn't take me long to finish it. I washed it down with orange juice while Abby stood at the kitchen counter watching as I ate. When I finished, I cleaned the table and took my empty glass over to the sink. Like a gentleman.

She made a face as I put the glass away and said, "You need to shower and shave. While you're doing that, I'm going to Walmart to get a few things. You need anything?"

The day before, we'd stopped at the same Walmart. Before we'd gone in, she'd asked me the same question. I hadn't needed anything then, and nothing had changed. I said, "No, I'm fine. I've got everything I need. Except a few hours of sleep."

I dug into my pocket and fished out the motorhome keys. "You'll need these when you get back."

She took the keys and headed out. I locked the door behind her and sat back down on the couch. I didn't think I needed a shower. I'd taken a quick one the night before. But I'd been pepper sprayed and handcuffed since then and hadn't cleaned up. I hadn't shaved since leaving Florida.

Since Abby and I were living in close quarters and since

she'd said I needed to shower and shave, I decided I probably should. I turned on the hot water heater and went back to the bedroom to get some clean clothes. I gave Bob a few pets and then went over to the bathroom. I stripped off and stepped into the shower stall.

It was then that I remembered where I kept Bob's litter box—on the floor of the stall. It was the perfect spot for his box and one of the few places in the motorhome where it wasn't in the way. Behind the shower curtain, it was out of sight, yet easy for Bob to get to. The closed curtain gave him privacy and meant we didn't have to look at his never empty litter box every time we went into the bathroom.

As long as I remembered to move it before I stepped into the shower, all was well.

I had remembered to move it the night before when I took a shower to clean the mud off from Crystal Mountain. And I'd remembered to put it back after the shower.

But being sleepy and maybe in a hurry to comply with Abby's shower directive, I'd completely forgotten about the litter box. When I stepped into the shower, the box was still there and I stepped into the litter and onto the fresh deposits Bob had left in it overnight.

As soon as my foot squished into his droppings, I realized my mistake. But it was too late. His fresh poo was oozing up between my toes.

Not wanting to spread the mess onto the floor, I stepped out of the shower and stood on one leg while bracing myself on the bathroom vanity.

In the process of doing that, I bumped the bathroom door with my elbow, right on my funny bone, sending a shock wave through my body. Forgetting I was standing on one foot and bracing myself on the vanity, I reached around with my free arm to rub my elbow.

That caused me to lose my balance. To keep from falling, I hopped out the bathroom and into the hall. Normally, that wouldn't have been a problem. I live alone, and Bob would have been the only one who would have seen me standing naked in the hall hopping on one foot while using my free hand to rub my throbbing elbow.

But as it turned out, Abby had decided she really didn't need anything from Walmart and had come back to the motorhome. I didn't hear her when she tapped the door, nor did I hear her when she came in. Had I, I could have hopped into the bathroom, closed the door behind me and everything would have been fine. But it wasn't.

When she walked in, I was naked and hopping on one foot while rubbing my elbow with my free hand. My other foot was covered with cat poo.

From behind me, I heard her ask, "Is this what you do when I leave? You get naked, smear poo on your body and do some kind of weird dance?"

Before I could answer, she said, "Say cheese."

Instead of helping me, she was taking pictures. And laughing.

Chapter Thirty-Seven

I hopped back into the bathroom, closing the door behind me. I grabbed some toilet paper and used it to wipe the poo from my foot. Then I grabbed the litter box and set it on the toilet.

With the shower stall cleared, I turned on the water, stepped in and took a long, hot shower. After that, I shaved, not looking forward to seeing Abby and explaining why she'd seen me hopping around naked.

After shaving, I put the litter box back in the shower, put on clean clothes and headed out to face the music and laughter.

As it turned out, Abby had already figured out what had happened. Instead of asking me about it, all she said was, "The litter box? You forgot to move it, right?"

I nodded. "Yeah. I stepped right in it."

She smiled. "You probably won't forget next time."

She was right, I probably wouldn't forget to move the box in the future. And that was the end of the conversation.

She was sitting at the kitchen table with the road atlas opened in front of her. She tapped a page and said, "It's an easy drive from here. We go north on 7 for two miles. Turn left on 298 and stay on it until we get to the Fish Village sign. It's about thirty miles from here. Probably take an hour.

"I'll go first in the Jeep and you follow me. I'm ready to leave whenever you are."

I'd eaten breakfast, showered, shaved and taken care of my normal morning business. We'd boon-docked in the Walmart parking lot which meant no hookups to worry about, no slide room to bring in. All I needed was a bottle of water and I was ready to hit the road.

After grabbing a water, I took my place into the driver's seat and said, "I'm ready. Lead the way."

Abby went out to her Jeep and let it warm up for about a minute, then gave me a thumbs up, signaling she was ready to go. I'd started the motorhome when she'd started the Jeep, and I was ready to roll.

Leaving the parking lot, we took a right and stayed on highway 7 north until we got to 298 where we took a left. It was a two-lane blacktop and in pretty good condition considering it ran through the backwoods of Arkansas.

Had I been driving a car, the rolling hills and sweeping curves through the semi-mountainous terrain would have been fun, but in a motorhome not so much. There were no shoulders, no passing lanes and no turn-offs.

The motorhome slowed at each hill, leaned to the side on each curve and just barely fit between the lines on the narrow road. It was a far cry from driving the flat and wide super highways of Florida.

Fortunately, there was no traffic. No cars stacking up behind me, no one trying to pass. Just Abby in front, in her green Jeep, and me bringing up the rear.

Forty minutes later, at the intersection of 298 and 27, we rolled up to a stop sign in the little town of Story, Arkansas. Population nine hundred fifty-seven. I counted five buildings,—two churches, a post office, a gas station and the Bluebell Cafe and Feed store.

According to the sign on the Bluebell, they had the best

burgers around. I figured since they were the only place we'd seen where you could get a burger for thirty miles, their claim was probably legit. The number of cars in the parking lot attested to either the quality of their food or the lack of competition.

I was hoping that after we got set up at the campground we could come back and give their burgers a try.

Abby pulled away from the stop sign, took a left on highway 27 and I followed. Six miles later, after crossing the bridge over the Ouachita River, we saw the 27 Fish Village sign. Abby turned and followed it to where the road changed from pavement to gravel.

The gravel marked the entrance to the campground, a collection of rough cabins, mobile homes and camping sites for anglers wanting to try their luck on the nearby river. Since Abby was in front and in the smaller vehicle, she pulled up to the office and got out. Before going in, she waved me over to the far side of the narrow road, moving me out of the way of a pickup truck pulling a boat that had stopped behind me.

The driver of the truck waved as he went around and the two teenaged boys in the back, both wearing matching Arkansas Razorback ball caps, also waved as the truck passed.

My first impression was everyone at the Fish Village seemed pretty friendly. In a lot of places, no one waves, except maybe with a middle finger.

When Abby came out of the office, she was carrying a registration packet and signaled me to follow her. She got into her Jeep, pulled away from the office, and headed down the road that led to the RV sites. Along the way, we passed a few mobile homes, five red plank cabins, and three grass-covered tent sites.

None of the sites were paved, but they looked level and were spaced well apart.

Near the end of the loop road, Abby pulled over to the right and stopped. I didn't see a campsite, but I figured she knew what she was doing and since I was behind her I stopped as well.

She walked to my window and said, "This is our site, between those trees over there. It's kind of narrow, so you'll have to be careful when you back in. I'll move my Jeep out of the way and guide you."

Without waiting to see if I had any questions, she turned and went back to her Jeep. Had she waited, I could have asked if she was sure about our site because all I saw was a narrow, grass-covered gap between two large pine trees.

There was no marker saying it was a campsite, no number on a post, no tire tracks leading to a parking pad, just Abby's word that it was the site assigned to us.

I wasn't so sure she was right.

Rather than risk backing the motorhome into a tree or soft ground, I decided to get out and take a closer look. I killed the motor, stood up and headed for the door.

Abby was waiting for me outside. All smiles.

"Isn't this a great spot?"

I looked around, confused because I didn't see a campsite. Just trees. But since I didn't want to dampen her spirit, I said, "Show me."

She smiled, took my hand and said, "Follow me."

Chapter Thirty-Eight

Abby led me away from the spot where I thought we were supposed to camp and took me down a narrow path that went to the river. We passed a picnic bench and a fire ring on the way. When we got to the water's edge, she put her arm around my waist and said, "Isn't this nice?"

It *was* nice. We were standing on the bank of the Ouachita River, in the backwoods of Arkansas in the fall, surrounded by the blazing reds and yellows of the changing colors of the leaves. Cool, crisp air, untainted by smokestacks and chimneys. A long way from the sounds of civilization. No low-flying planes. No loud motorcycles, no boom, boom stereos.

Just the burble of the slow-moving water in front of us making its way east. It was peaceful, and if we weren't on a mission, I would have liked to sit on the rocks and watch the river go by. But we couldn't do that. Not yet.

We needed to set up camp and go find Kat. After that, we'd have time to come back to the river and relax.

Abby could sense my impatience. She said, "Okay, enough with the scenic tour. Time to get the motorhome parked and go see Kat."

She grabbed my hand and led me back up the path to the level ground across from where I had parked the RV. She stopped at the picnic table on the river side of the road, directly across from where I thought we were going to camp.

"This is our site. Here. There's plenty of room for your motorhome. You'll just have to back up slowly and stop before you get to the slope leading down to the river. Get in, I'll guide you."

She walked over to the picnic table and waited for me to start the motorhome. As soon as she heard it rumble to life, she moved over and stood where I could see her in my mirror.

I eased my foot off the brake and followed her hand signals to get into the site. When she held both palms up, followed by a cutting motion across her throat, I killed the motor and set the brake.

While I was doing that, she walked up to my window and said, "You might want to check to make sure the slide room will clear."

I trusted her judgment but decided to get out and look anyway. It would cost thousands if I ran the slide into a tree or picnic table.

I got out and followed her to the back of the site. She pointed to the slide and asked, "What do you think?"

Even though there were no painted lines showing where the site started or stopped, the motorhome was perfectly positioned on the narrow gravel pad. The rear tires were a foot from the end of the gravel, the utility compartment was lined up with park's power pedestal, and there was plenty of room to extend the slide.

I nodded and said, "Good job. I couldn't have done it without you."

She smiled and said, "You're right. You couldn't have done it without me. That's why we make a good team. You and me. Together."

She pointed at the power pedestal. "You get us hooked

up, I'll go inside and get things ready."

As she walked away, I thought about what she'd said about us making a good team. We'd only known each other for two days, but so far it had worked out well.

Having her around felt good, which was a strange feeling for me. I'd spent a lot of time living alone in the motorhome and had gotten used to not having anyone else around. But with Abby, it was different. Life with her had been interesting and drama free. At least so far.

I got us connected to shore power and went back inside. She was waiting for me, sitting on the couch with Bob in her lap. His little stub of a tail twitched side to side. He was enjoying the attention she was giving him. She rubbed his ears and said, "I'll take him to the back while you run the slide out."

She knew Bob didn't need to be anywhere near the wall when it was moving. He could be crushed if he were in the wrong place at the wrong time. She picked him up and headed to the back and as soon as I heard the bedroom door close, I took care of the slide and called out, "Okay, it's safe."

When she came back up front, she pointed at the couch and said, "Want me to open some windows?"

I did. In fact, opening the windows was exactly what I was thinking when she asked the question. I wasn't sure whether her asking it was a coincidence or something related to her 'gift'. It didn't matter; she already knew the answer.

She opened the windows up front, and I did the ones in the back. To increase air flow, I opened the two Fantastic fan ceiling vents—the one over the couch and the one in the hall.

With the windows and vents open, the cool mountain air would keep it comfortable inside for Bob while we were gone. He could hop up onto the back of the couch, lean up against the window screen, and spy on the birds and squirrels outside. It was one of his most favorite things to do, and as soon as the windows were open, he did it.

Abby beamed like a proud parent when Bob jumped up on the back of the couch, and stretched out against the screen. His chirps of joy brought smiles all around.

We watched him for a few moments, then Abby turned to me and said, "We need to get over to the crystal mine and see if we can find Kat. You go wash up, and I'll grab a couple bottles of water and meet you in the Jeep."

She headed outside, and I went back and checked Bob's food, water and litter box. His food was a little low, so I topped it off with his favorite dry mix. The litter box needed tending to again, but that would have to wait until we came back. I washed my hands, combed my hair, locked up the motorhome and went outside.

Abby was waiting for me, sitting on the hood of her Jeep. She was wearing faded jeans over tan hiking boots. A white button up fishing shirt, a dark blue ball cap pulled down tight, a short ponytail out the back. Dark sun glasses and a smile pulled it all together.

It was a great look for her, one that wouldn't have been out of place on the cover of an Eddie Bauer or Columbia Outdoor catalog. A beautiful girl waiting for her next big adventure.

I probably stared at her a bit too long because she cocked her head and mouthed the word, "What?"

I was pretty sure she knew why I was staring. She looked good and she knew it.

She slid down off the Jeep and said, "Let's go."

Chapter Thirty-Nine

The Sweet Surrender Crystal Mine was six miles north of our campsite at the Highway 27 Fish Village. Abby knew the way. She'd asked about it when she'd registered at the campground and they told her how to get there. They warned her that the road, the one they called Horseshoe Bend, was dirt and would be muddy after the previous day's rain. But since she was in a Jeep, she shouldn't worry, at least about that part.

The challenge would be when she got to the Sweet Surrender turnoff and took the road up the hill to the mine. They said it wasn't really a road, more like a logging trail the mine owners had carved up the mountain. Not paved, not gravel, just dirt. After a good rain, it might be impassable. Even without rain, four-wheel drive was recommended.

Abby said she wasn't worried. She'd already driven her Jeep up a muddy mountain road in heavy rain and knew what it could do. As far as she was concerned, her little green Jeep could go anywhere.

When we got to the Sweet Surrender turnoff and saw the deep ruts going up the hill, she rolled the Jeep to a stop, shifted into four-wheel drive and said, "No problem."

She steered toward the middle of the muddy track and eased the Jeep up the hill. I held on and watched her instead of the road ahead. She had both hands on the wheel, a smile on her face and she looked like was enjoying the adventure. If anything, she looked disappointed when we reached the top of the hill where the road ended in a parking lot. She wanted the ride to last a little longer.

There were four other cars already in the lot. Two four-wheel drive pickups, a newer looking Land Rover and a primer gray Nissan Pathfinder. The right rear passenger window on the Pathfinder was covered with plastic and duct tape. A faded sticker with the words "Git-R-Done" hung from the rear bumper.

Abby saw it first. "Isn't that Digger's?"

I nodded. "Yeah, looks like it. Wonder what he's doing here."

She laughed. "Maybe he's looking for suckers to buy his secret crystal maps. Like we did."

I grunted. She was right. I had forked over a hundred dollars for a map he was selling to others for twenty bucks. I'd been taken and should have been mad.

But the map had led us to Crystal Mountain, and according to the woman we'd found there in the rain, led to museum quality crystals. The one she had given to Abby was wrapped in newspaper in the Jeep's glove compartment. It was the nicest I'd ever seen.

The parking lot of Sweet Surrender wasn't paved, parking spots weren't marked and it looked like you could park anywhere you wanted. Abby figured Digger had been to the mine before and knew the best place, so she pulled over and parked next to his Pathfinder.

I started to get out, but she stopped me and said, "If we find Kat, go along with whatever I say. No matter what it is, go along with it. Okay?"

I nodded. "Sure, no problem."

She reached into her pocket and pulled out the wedding

ring she had put on two days earlier. She put it on her finger and said, "This is going to be part of our story. Put yours on."

She had given me a wedding band when we first met, and I'd worn it until we left the casino. I couldn't remember where I had taken it off or where it had ended up, but I didn't have it on my finger.

I shrugged and said, "Sorry, but I don't know where the ring is."

She pointed a finger at me and said, "When we get married for real, I won't abide by you losing your ring. You'll wear it all the time. You understand?"

I figured she was joking, so I went along. "Yes dear. When we're married, I won't lose the ring and I'll wear it all the time."

She smiled, reached into her pocket and pulled out the missing wedding band and handed it to me. "Put it on and don't take it off until we get back to Florida."

I took the ring but didn't put it on right away. I didn't mind wearing it for a few hours if it helped us find Kat, but no way was I going to wear it until we got back to Florida.

I didn't tell Abby this, though. No need to upset her. I put the ring on and showed it to her on my finger.

She smiled and said, "Good." Then she pointed at Digger's car. "He didn't go into the mine. He's over there under that tree, smoking a cigarette. Why don't you go talk to him, see what he's up to while I go look for Kat"

She got out of the Jeep and headed toward a woman wearing a straw hat carrying a clipboard. I got out on the other side and walked across the dirt parking lot toward Digger.

He watched as I walked toward him but didn't say

anything until I got close. When he did speak, he said, "You followed the map up to Crystal Mountain?"

I nodded. "Yeah, we did. Went up there at night, in the rain."

"You find anything?"

"Yeah, we found a woman who'd bought your map. She said she paid twenty dollars for it."

He nodded. "She find any crystals?"

"Yeah, she did. Some pretty nice ones."

He smiled. "I told you the map would lead you to crystals."

I motioned toward his car. "What brings you out here? Trying to sell more maps?"

He took a drag on his cigarette, held it in, and then blew out a smoke ring and coughed out his answer. "They won't let me go in there, won't let me sell my maps either. I've been banned."

I could understand why. If I owned the place and someone like Digger showed up trying to sell maps that made customers want to go somewhere else, I'd ban him too.

Still, he had come to the mine, and I wanted to know why. "You drove all the way out here, but you can't dig crystals, and you can't sell maps. Seems a long way to go for things you can't do."

He casually pointed to the graded field where a few people were searching for crystals. "Your friend over there paid me to bring him here. Fifty bucks each way and all I had to do was drive."

His answer surprised me. As far as I knew, I didn't have any friends in this part of the country.

"My friend? You sure about that?"

He nodded. "Yeah, the guy who was with Kat. He paid me to bring him out here. Said he needed to talk to her and he knew she was here. The money was good, so I drove him. When he gets done talking, I'm going to drive him back.

"Meanwhile, I'm going to sit here on this rock and smoke another cigarette. You're welcome to join me."

Chapter Forty

I passed on the offer to smoke with Digger. Instead, I headed to the mine hoping to find Abby before she ran into Kat and Dylan.

I wanted to give her a heads-up so she could adjust her story if needed. But as I walked toward the mine, I was stopped by the woman with the clipboard and straw hat, the same one Abby had talked to. She smiled and said, "Before you go in, you have to register and pay."

I pointed to Abby. "I'm with her, the woman you just talked to. Abby. She should have registered for both of us."

The woman look confused. "Abby? I thought her name was Paige."

"Oh right. Paige. Don't tell her I called her the wrong name. She'll get mad."

The woman smiled knowingly. "Old girlfriend's name? The new ones always get mad when you call them the old name."

She tapped her clipboard. "You must be Tony, her husband. She said you'd be coming over. She said to tell you she left her purse in the car and for you to pay. But there's no need for that. Being that you folks are on your honeymoon, we don't want your money. You and your wife can have free access to the mine all day long."

I started to say something about us not being married, and certainly not on our honeymoon, but figured it was best not to go against Abby's story. I thanked the woman and headed into the mine.

When you hear the word mine, you probably think of a dark tunnel leading to a deep hole in the ground with old timbers supporting the roof and water seeping through. Some mines are like that. But not crystal mines.

Instead of a dark hole going into the ground, crystal mines are usually open fields of cleared and plowed forest lands. Visitors dig through piles of tailings cut from the crystal rich seams.

Serious hunters will bring digging tools, screwdrivers or small shovels, and dig through the tailings, but most visitors just walk around picking up crystals they find on the ground.

According to the lady with the clipboard, recent visitors to Sweet Surrender were finding nice clusters and some large points. She said that most were coated with iron, giving them a dark color until they were cleaned. She said to bring anything we found back to her, and she'd show us how to clean them.

I wasn't interested in digging or cleaning crystals. I wanted to find Abby and Kat, and with so few people working in the mine that early in the morning, it was easy to spot them. Two women standing close to each other and next to them, a man I presumed to be Dylan.

He was about six feet tall, had longish blond hair, and was wearing faded jeans and a black T-shirt. He wasn't carrying digging tools or a finds basket, which meant he probably didn't come to dig crystals.

I walked toward them, and when Kat saw me, she broke out into a big smile. She ran over to me, gave me a hug and said, "I can't believe you're getting married. You're the last person I figured would tie the knot.

"But you picked a good one. Abby is just perfect for you."

I wasn't sure what she meant by that, Abby being perfect for me. It could have been a compliment or maybe not. It really didn't matter though; Abby and I weren't really getting married. It was a ruse she had cooked up. I didn't know the reason behind it, but I went along with it. It was easier that way.

I smiled and said, "I never thought I'd get married either, but then I met Abby and things changed."

Kat looked at me and shook her head. "Never thought it would happen."

Abby came over and put her arm around my waist, trying to make us look like a real couple. I leaned in and kissed her on the cheek, helping to sell the illusion.

Dylan stepped over to me and said, "You must be Walker. Kat has told me all about you. You still living in a motorhome?"

I nodded. "Yeah, I am. But that'll probably change, what with me getting married and all."

Out of the corner of my eye, I saw Abby and Kat take a few steps back. They started talking to each other in a whisper.

Dylan either didn't see them move away or didn't care. He was more interested in talking to me. He said, "You live in Florida?"

I nodded. "Yeah, I do. Near Sarasota."

He didn't seem surprised. Kat had probably already told him where I lived. His next question was unexpected.

"You heading back soon? In your motorhome?"

"Yeah, probably in a few days."

He looked around, then asked, "You got room for an extra person?"

It was a strange question, especially to ask of a man who was supposedly on his honeymoon. I thought about it before I answered, then said, "If I were traveling alone, there'd be plenty of room. But not this time. Not with Abby and me on our honeymoon.

"You looking for a ride back to Florida?"

He said, "Yeah I am. Kat said she's not going back anytime soon, and I have business I need to attend to."

"Business? What kind of business you in?"

He reached into his pocket and pulled out a small crystal. "I sell these to the tourists in Key West. Came up here to restock and now that I've got a full load, I need to get back."

I nodded, having learned from the deputy more about his real business than Dylan probably wanted me to know.

"So, you're going back soon? When you leaving?"

He nodded toward Kat. "Soon as I get her to unlock the motorhome so I can get my backpack. It's got my money and ID in it."

Upon hearing us talk about her, Kat and Abby rejoined us. She said, "I heard my name. You two talking about me?"

I shook my head. "Not me. I know better."

She turned to Dylan. "What'd you say about me? Fess up."

He pointed with his thumb over his shoulder to the parking lot where Digger was waiting. "I told him the same thing I told you, that I need you to unlock your motorhome so I can get my backpack. Then I'm heading to Florida."

Kat didn't seem surprised with his answer. She just

nodded and said, "You know you'll have to go without me. I'm staying here for a while."

He smiled. "No problem. Stay as long as you want. I just need to get in your RV for a minute. I'll grab my pack and be on my way. Give me a key, and I'll let myself in."

She shook her head and said, "I came here to dig crystals. I'm not going back to the motorhome today, and I'm not going to give you a key."

She reached over and took Abby's hand and they walked away.

Dylan turned to me. "I need to get into her motorhome. Think you might be able to change her mind?"

I shrugged. "I don't know. But I'll try. You stay here; I'll go talk to her."

I walked away, leaving him standing alone in the middle of the crystal mine. If he thought anything was up, he didn't show it.

Chapter Forty-One

Abby and Kat had moved far enough away so that Dylan wouldn't be able to hear their conversation. I went over to join them.

The first thing I said was, "You know what he wants."

Kat nodded. "Yeah, he wants to get into the motorhome."

"And he doesn't have a key."

Kat turned away so Dylan couldn't read her lips. She said, "I don't have my keys. I gave them to the deputy."

Apparently, Abby had told Kat we had spoken to the deputy and that we knew what was up with Dylan.

Kat shook her head. "I can't go to the motorhome with him. He got me into this mess, and I'm so mad I might just finish him off. Then dump his body in the woods where no one would ever find him."

She could have been kidding, but there was a good chance she wasn't. Being the daughter of a Russian Mafia boss, she had been trained to do things like making people disappear without a trace. She could do it if she wanted to. No problem.

Abby could see that Kat was getting worked up, so she leaned in and whispered, "There's no need to kill anyone. We've got this under control."

She reached into her pocket and pulled out the key she hadn't given the deputy. The key that opened the side door.

"Give him this. Tell him to use it to get in the motorhome and leave it at the campground office."

Kat looked surprised. "You have a key? You didn't give it to the deputy?"

Abby shook her head. "I gave her a key but not all of them. I thought it'd be a good idea to keep at least one."

She put it in Kat's hand. "This will unlock the side door but won't start the motor. He can use it to get in, but he can't use it to drive away."

Kat understood. "So, I give this to Dylan. He uses it to get in. Then what?"

Abby reached into her shirt pocket and pulled out the business card the deputy had given her that morning. "When you give him the key, and he leaves with Digger, we call the deputy and let her know he's on his way. Then we spend the rest of the day here, digging crystals.

"When we get hungry, we'll send Walker over to the Bluebell and have him bring us lunch.

"Then, if things are not wrapped up by the end of the day, you can spend the night with us. We're camped about five miles from here."

I looked over my shoulder and saw that Dylan was still standing where I left him. In the middle of the mine. Just looking around like he had no worries in the world. He saw me look in his direction and he nodded. I gave him a thumbs up, and he smiled.

He started to walk toward us, but I shook my head. Not yet. He got the message and stopped.

I turned to Kat. "It's up to you. Either give him the key or tell him to go away. If you don't give him the key, my guess is he'll go back to your motorhome and break in. Probably knock out a window.

"If he does that, you won't be able to drive it until you get it fixed. If it rains, it'll be trouble."

She thought about it for a moment, then said, "You two stay here. I'll go talk to him."

Abby and I stood our ground as we watched Kat walk over to Dylan. She spoke a few words, handed him the key and they hugged. He waved in our direction and walked away. Happy and carefree.

Kat watched until he was out of the mine area and then she came back to us. She was shaking her head. "That bastard. He really messed things up. He could have taken me down with him."

Abby nodded. "He could have. But he didn't. Now that he's gone, let's go over to my car and catch up on a few things."

We left the mine area and walked over to Abby's green Jeep. When we got close, Kat said, "This is yours? How cute! When did you get it?"

Abby told her how we had found the Jeep for sale just outside of Hot Springs and how she had always wanted one and, when she saw it, she just had to have it.

We piled inside, with Abby and Kat in the front and me in the back. Kat drummed her hands on the dash and asked, "Where we going?"

Abby shook her head. "Nowhere. Not until we make a call."

She held out her phone. "You want me to call the deputy or do you want to do it?"

Kat shook her head. "You call. I'm afraid I might say the wrong thing."

Abby pulled the deputy's card out of her pocket and called the handwritten number on the back. When the call ended, she filled us in.

"She said they'll have someone watching the motorhome. They won't try to bust him while he's inside. They'll wait till he walks out and has the stuff on him.

"She said none of us should go over there until she calls back and says it's clear."

Kat thought about it for a minute and then reached out for Abby's phone. Her own phone was still back in her motorhome, and she wanted to make a call. But Abby wouldn't let her. Not before asking a question. "Who you want to call?"

Kat smiled. "My dad. He needs to know where I am."

Abby said, "Good. He'll be happy to hear from you."

But she didn't give Kat her phone. Instead, she made the call herself and when Kat's father answered, she said, "I'm sitting here next to your daughter. Would you like to speak to her?"

Chapter Forty-Two

When Kat took the phone, Abby and I stepped out of the Jeep, giving her some privacy while she spoke with her father.

The call lasted about ten minutes; we couldn't hear much of it. We did hear her say she was safe, and was sorry she hadn't called earlier and let him know where she was.

It didn't sound like she told him about the problem with Dylan or the drugs. Her father wouldn't have been happy hearing about that and might have wanted to get some of his heavy hitters involved. It was probably good she hadn't mentioned it.

She ended the call, promising to call again the next day and tell him more. She climbed out of the Jeep and handed the phone back to Abby. Then she asked, "You two really getting married?"

I started to answer with an emphatic, "No," but Abby stopped me.

She grabbed my hand and said, "It's complicated. Walker here isn't sure what he wants. But I am."

Maybe she was kidding. Or maybe she wasn't. I was still wearing her ring and maybe she really thought we were getting married. I sure hoped not.

Then she said, "What I want right now is one of those burgers from the Bluebell back in Story."

She turned to me. "What about you, Walker? You

hungry?"

I was. A burger sounded good. A lot better than getting married, so I said, "Yeah, let's go get food."

We piled into Abby's Jeep and headed to the Bluebell. Along the way, Kat told us she had been staying in a guest cabin on the mine grounds. The cabins usually weren't available, but when the deputy flashed her badge, the mine manager said that Kat could stay in one for a few days. It was rustic, but liveable.

The parking lot at the Blue Bell was almost full when we got there. Eight pickup trucks and a tractor. Fortunately, the tractor was just leaving when we pulled in.

Inside, a sign said, "Seat yourself. " We looked around and found an open table by the window and claimed it. Almost immediately, a young girl in jeans came over to take our order. We all wanted the same thing, burger, fries and a Coke.

Ten minutes later, our food came and when it did, it met the promise on the sign painted outside. The best burger around. There was no doubt about it. The burger was good, the fries were fresh cut and tasty, and the Coke was ice cold.

We ate, talked about the last few days, and after everyone was through, I paid. I left a ten-dollar tip on the table, and instead of heading back to the mine, we went to our campsite at the Fish Village.

Kat was tired and wanted to rest and Abby thought the motorhome would be a better place for a nap than the parking lot at the crystal mine.

Bob met us at the door. He rubbed up against Abby's ankles and did the same with Kat, who he had met on an earlier trip. When I stepped in, he ran from me over to Abby. I guess he preferred her over me. I didn't blame him. She petted him more than I did.

When Abby sat on the couch, he jumped up beside her and rubbed his head against her arm. Before long, he was in her lap, purring.

Kat had gone to the back to wash up. When she came back up front, she said, "I have a funny feeling about this."

Abby nodded. "I do too. Something seems off."

I thought for a moment then asked Kat, "When the deputy searched your motorhome and found pills, did she show them to you?"

She shook her head. "No, she didn't. She said the pills were laced with fentanyl and we shouldn't touch them."

I nodded. "After she found the pills, did she keep searching or did she stop?"

"She stopped. She said that was all she needed."

"How long did it take her to find the pills once she got inside your motorhome?"

"About two minutes. She went straight into the bedroom and came out saying she'd found pills."

"But you never saw any pills, right?"

"Right, I never saw any pills."

"Did Dylan ever do anything that made you think he was using or selling Oxy?"

She shook her head. "That's the thing. He didn't act like someone on pills. He never said anything about drugs and never tried to hide his backpack. The only thing he seemed interested in doing was finding crystals to take back to Florida. "

I nodded and continued my questions. "Is it possible that he's clean? That maybe there weren't any pills? And maybe

255

the deputy made it all up?"

Kat shook her head. "Why would she do that? Why go to the trouble of getting me out of the motorhome just so she could bust Dylan for not having pills?"

Abby had stayed out of it until the question about the deputy came up. At that point, she had something to say. "What if she really isn't a deputy?"

I shook my head. "She showed you her badge, right? Right after she maced me, she showed you her badge."

Abby nodded. "Yeah, she did. And it looked real. But maybe it wasn't. Do you remember her last name?"

I didn't, but Kat did. "Moretti. That's her last name."

Abby pulled out her phone and looked up the Garland County Sheriff's Office. She found the number and made the call. We could only hear her side of the conversation. It went something like this:

"Yes, I'd like to speak to Deputy Moretti."

"Correct, Moretti."

"I spoke to her earlier, and need to update her on a case she's working on."

"Yes, this morning."

"Okay, I'll hold."

There were a few moments of silence, then, "Yes, I'm calling to speak to Deputy Moretti."

"This morning."

"Red hair, stocky build, about five foot ten."

"Really? When?"

"I'm sorry to hear that."

"Yes, she showed me her ID and badge."

"Right now? She's probably going to the Crystal Ridge campground where the motorhome is parked."

"She has the keys. I gave them to her."

"She said it was a drug investigation and she had a warrant for Dylan Lancaster."

There was a pause, then:

"Really, no warrant? Nothing on Dylan?"

"Good to know. But what about the woman?"

"I understand. We'll meet you there."

She ended the call and said, "We need to go to Kat's motorhome. Right now. I'll tell you why on the way."

She grabbed the keys to her Jeep and headed out the door. Kat and I followed.

Chapter Forty-Three

Abby was driving the Jeep and telling us about her call with the sheriff's office. She said, "When I asked to speak to Deputy Moretti, I could tell there was a problem. They asked me twice if I was sure I had the name right. They wanted to be certain it was Moretti I was working with. I assured them it was.

"That's when they put me on hold. A few seconds later, a man picked up. He said he was the sheriff and wanted me to confirm I had spoken to Moretti. I told him we had spoken to her a few hours earlier and she had shown us her badge and ID.

"He wanted me to describe the deputy and I did. That's when he told me the real Deputy Moretti had been killed three months earlier. Her body had been found in the woods, minus her ID, badge and gun.

"Since then, a woman matching the description I gave had been using Moretti's badge to impersonate her and rip off tourists. The sheriff's office had been trying to find the woman so they could question her about a number of crimes, including the real deputy's death.

"The Sheriff said if the fake deputy had the keys to the motorhome, chances were good she planned to steal it. The only way to stop her was to get to the motorhome before she took off in it. He was sending two cars and said if we got there first, detain her if we could."

It was about twenty-eight miles from the Fish Village to the Crystal Ridge RV park. With Abby driving the Jeep flat out, it would take us at least thirty minutes to get there on the narrow mountain roads.

We were halfway there when I popped open the Jeep's glove compartment and pulled out the map we had bought from Digger. I was hoping he had put his phone number on it somewhere. But he hadn't.

Kat, who was sitting in the back seat, saw the map and said, "I've got one of those. Got it from Digger."

I nodded. "He told us he gave you one. Any chance he wrote his phone number on yours?"

She smiled. "Yeah, in fact he did. But I left my phone in the RV and couldn't call him. I've got the map if you want to see it."

She pulled it out her pocket and handed it to me. Near the bottom of the page, below the driving directions, a phone number had been scrawled in pencil.

I pulled out my phone and called it.

After three rings, Digger answered.

"This is Digger."

"Digger, this is Walker. Saw you this morning at Sweet Surrender. Remember me?"

"Yeah, I remember. What do you want?"

"Kat's motorhome. Next to yours. Is it still there?"

"Hold on. I'll look."

I heard him take a few steps and open a door. A few seconds later, he came back on line.

"Yeah, it's still there. Looks like somebody's in it though. The door's wide open. Yeah, I can see her now. There's a woman going in. A big woman. Carrying a duffel bag.

"She's not alone. There are two guys with her. Young fella and an older man. Looks like they're in a hurry to get on the road."

He paused, then said, "Yep, they're fixing to leave. Guy outside went around to unhook and the other guy just started the motor."

This was bad news. We were at least ten minutes away, and if the Sheriff didn't get there in time, Kat's motorhome would be long gone before anyone could stop it.

Digger was our only hope.

I filled him in on what was going on. "Digger, they're trying to steal Kat's motorhome. The cops are on the way but may not get there in time. I need you to keep those people from leaving in it."

There was a pause as Digger thought about what I had said.

"You're sure they're stealing it? I saw them go in. They had a key."

"Yeah Digger, I'm sure they're stealing it. Kat's with me. They stole her keys and are trying to take her motorhome."

He got serious. "That ain't good. What you want me to do?"

"Block them in. Move your car over and park in front so they can't go anywhere. Make it so they can't leave. Think you can do that?"

"I'll try. I'll call you back in a minute."

He ended the call.

I turned to Kat. "You heard that, right?"

She nodded.

261

"Good. Digger says they're over at your motorhome right now, getting ready to leave in it. He's going to try to stop them."

We were five minutes out when the first state trooper went around us. Two minutes later, two more cops went past, both in a hurry.

By the time we reached the campground, it was all over. Patrol cars surrounded Kat's motorhome. Four people stood in front, in cuffs. One of them was Digger.

Abby tried to pull the Jeep up close, but her way was blocked by patrol car. She pulled up to it and started to get out, but a trooper walked over, his hand on his holster, and said, "Sorry miss, this area is closed."

She nodded. "We know. We're the ones who called the sheriff about the fake deputy."

She pointed to Kat in the backseat. "It's her motorhome they were trying to steal."

The trooper nodded, pulled out his walkie talkie and spoke a few words. After hearing a response, he came back to Abby's window and said, "Park over there. By the restrooms. Don't get out of your car until an officer arrives."

Abby did as she was told. She pulled into the parking space in front of the campground showers and killed the motor. Seeing the number and intensity of the police and all the guns they were carrying, we decided it would be best to stay in the car until we were told to get out.

Thirty minutes later, an officer walked up and tapped the roof of the Jeep with his flashlight. He asked, "Which one of you is Katrina Chesnokov?"

From the backseat, Kat said, "I am."

The officer leaned over to see who had spoken and then

said, "Okay Katrina, get out. You other two stay in there until I come back."

Kat got out, and she and the officer walked toward her motorhome. They spoke as they walked, but neither Abby nor I could hear what was being said.

When they got to where Digger stood with his hands cuffed behind his back, Kat pointed at him and said something to the officer. Another officer came over and spoke with her at length. A few minutes later, he instructed one of the uniformed cops to uncuff Digger.

As soon as he was unhooked, Digger made a beeline for his trailer. He didn't come back out until all the police had gone.

Twenty minutes later, the same officer that had walked off with Kat came and got Abby. They walked away, leaving me behind. The only thing he said to me was, "Don't get out of the car and don't leave."

Ten minutes later, it was my turn. The same officer came and got me. Instead of taking me to Kat's motorhome, he took me to his car and had me lean up against the back bumper while he asked me questions.

Most were about our meeting with the fake deputy. A few were about where were we staying, how long we would be in town and why we hadn't called the sheriff's office sooner.

My guess was he had asked Kat and Abby the same questions. I answered truthfully. No reason not to.

Two hours later, it was all over. The police had arrested the fake deputy and her two accomplices. They had searched the motorhome and had found no drugs. They did find suitcases belonging to the people they had arrested and took those as evidence.

After checking everything, they released the motorhome

back to Kat. They gave her the keys the fake deputy had used, and had her sign a statement about what had happened. They told her to stay in town for a few days in case any questions came up.

When the last police car drove off, Digger came out of his trailer, cold beer in hand. He was wearing a clean T-shirt and a smile. He came over to where we were standing and said, "They didn't arrest me. I'm pretty proud about that."

He pointed to his Pathfinder, which was still parked in front of Kat's motorhome. The bumper of the RV was embedded along the entire length of the SUV's driver's side.

"I pulled in lengthwise so they couldn't go around. They yelled and hollered and cussed, but I wasn't going to move. They finally tried to push it out of their way, but all they did was dent up the side a bit. I'll probably have to take a hammer to it to get them doors to open."

I nodded, thinking it might take a lot more than a hammer to fix his broken down SUV. The motorhome's bumper had done a lot of damage. Not only were the front fender, driver's and rear passenger's doors pushed in, but the rear quarter panel of Digger's Pathfinder was pushed up tight up against the back tire.

It would take a lot of body work before the Pathfinder could be driven more than a few feet. Digger didn't seem to care, though. It had been a good day for him. He had made a hundred bucks driving Dylan to Sweet Surrender and back, had a twelve pack of cold beer in his fridge thanks to me and hadn't ended up in jail.

Kat walked over and gave him a hug. She smiled and said, "Digger, you saved my motorhome. It would have been long gone if you hadn't done what you did."

She looked at the crease down the side of his truck. "How

much you think it'll cost to fix that?"

He rubbed his chin and thought about it for a moment, then said, "It ain't worth fixing. As long as I can get the driver door to open and shut, it'll be good enough for me. Heck, the whole thing ain't worth more than five hundred dollars."

Kat pointed at Abby's green Jeep. "Would you trade it for that? Straight across?"

Digger looked at the Jeep and said, "Sure, I'd trade. Be a fool not to."

Kat nodded. "Tell you what. Abby has a friend who has another one just like it. What if I have them come up here and swap theirs for yours? It won't cost you a thing."

Digger shook his head. "I appreciate the offer, but you don't have to do that. I can hammer them dents out. When I get done, it'll be just like new."

Kat smiled. "Digger, listen to me. If it weren't for you, my motorhome would be long gone along with everything in it. I owe you big time. Let me pay you back. You want to trade for a Jeep or not?"

He took another sip from his beer, looked at his busted Pathfinder and said, "Yeah, let's trade. I'd be a fool not to."

Kat reached out and shook his hand. Then she asked Abby to call Grace and see if her brother would sell her another Jeep.

The call lasted about five minutes. When it was over, Abby filled us in.

"Grace said they had another Jeep ready to go. She said she could do the paperwork and have it up here in an hour. She also said her brother was ready to install the tow bar on my Jeep and can do it today if I want him to.

"I told her if she brought the Jeep she had for sale up to Kat's campsite, we could do the paperwork and she could take my Jeep back to the shop. Her brother could install the tow bar, and I'd pick it up later.

"She said that worked for her, and she'd be up here with the Jeep in an hour."

Kat was pleased to hear this. She said, "I better go check to see if I have enough cash to cover this."

She went in her motorhome, and Abby followed, leaving me and Digger outside.

We really didn't have much to talk about, but I did have a question. "What happened to Dylan? Where'd he go?"

Digger grunted out a half laugh, then said, "Nobody was in Kat's RV when we got here. Dylan used his key to go in and get his backpack. Then he came over to my place to have a beer and look at the crystals I had for sale.

"We were inside when I got your call, and when I told him what was going on and how the police were on their way, he grabbed his backpack and said, 'Dude, I'm bailing. Too much drama for me.'

"He left, but I didn't see where he went. I was too busy moving my truck, trying to keep them rascals from leaving in Kat's motorhome."

He paused for a moment then said, "I don't want to say anything bad about Dylan. He paid me the money he promised for driving him over to Sweet Surrender. And he bought about eight hundred dollars of crystals from me. He even paid me to ship them back to Florida FedEx. Said he'd spend more money with me next time."

I nodded, surprised to learn Dylan actually was in the business of buying and selling crystals and was probably a decent guy.

After that, Digger and I stood outside in silence, waiting for the girls to return. He was grinning like he'd won the lottery, and I didn't blame him. The Jeep he was getting was a lot better than the old Nissan he had been driving. He deserved a reward for sacrificing his car for people he hardly knew. Not many people would do that.

Chapter Forty-Four

As promised, Grace showed up with the Jeep within the hour. Like Abby's, it was Forest Service green, had four-wheel drive and in good condition. Unlike Digger's Nissan, all the windows were intact, the tires were new, and it didn't leave a trail of blue smoke as it went down the road.

Grace's brother arrived with her, and his first question to Abby was, "You buying another one?"

She shook her head and pointed at Kat. "I'm not buying it, she is."

He looked at Kat, smiled and said, "I'm Daniel. Nice to meet you."

Kat introduced herself and explained why she was buying the Jeep. Daniel was confused at first, but after Kat explained how Digger had helped save her motorhome, he understood.

With Digger's help, they wrote up a bill of sale, started the title transfer process and put a temporary plate on the back of the Jeep.

Daniel told Digger, "You have ten days to get it insured and registered. If you can't afford insurance, I know a guy who might give you five hundred dollars for your Pathfinder and you could put that toward insurance."

Digger shook his head. "You taking the Pathfinder in trade is part of this deal. I can't sell it. It belongs to you now."

Daniel smiled. "Don't take offense, but I don't want your

Pathfinder. It'll take up space in my shop, and it's not worth me fixing up. I don't have a problem with you selling it to my friend. He'll pay you cash for it and haul it off.

"Use the money to buy insurance and we'll all be happy."

Digger grinned. "Well, all right then. Tell your friend to come get it."

After the deal was struck and all the paperwork completed, Dan and Grace drove off in Abby's Jeep, promising to install the tow bar and have it ready to pull behind the motorhome on our way back to Florida.

Digger thanked Kat over and over and used the winch on his new-to-him Jeep to pull his Pathfinder away from her motorhome. He drug it to where it had been parked by his trailer and left it. He didn't bother locking the doors.

After thanking Kat a final time, he said he was going to drive his Jeep over to his ex-wife's place and take her and the kids for a ride. He left a happy man. That was the last we saw of him.

After he left, Abby asked Kat if she felt safe staying in her motorhome that night.

Kat said, "I'm not worried about being safe. I just don't want to deal with the drama if any of those people come back. I'd rather be somewhere else tonight."

Abby agreed. "I think it would be a good idea for you to move. Maybe over to Fish Village, next to us.

"Since Grace took our Jeep and we have no way to get back over there, we could ride with you in your motorhome."

Twenty minutes later, after unhooking from shore power, we left the campground in Kat's motorhome. She drove, Abby rode shotgun, and I sat in the back, watching the world go by.

On the way, Abby called Fish Village and reserved the spot next to ours for Kat. When we got there, she stopped at the office, paid and picked up her reservation packet. Then we went to her site and she backed right into it, no problem.

We decided that since the fridge in my motorhome was stocked with food and Kat's was empty, she would eat dinner with us.

Bob was happy for the company; his only problem was he couldn't decide which of the girls he liked best. He spent most of the evening moving between their laps, getting as many pets as he could.

After dinner and a box of wine, we turned in for the night. Kat in her motorhome, Abby in mine in my bed, and me on the sofa.

Sometime during the night, she joined me on the couch, and things got interesting.

Chapter Forty-Five

The next morning, just after seven, my phone rang with an incoming call. I was a bit groggy from the wine and really didn't want to answer it, but I did.

"This is Walker."

The voice on the other end said, "I should hope so. It's your phone. Who else would be answering it?"

The caller, a man, continued.

"Are you still in bed? If you are, I hope my daughter is not there with you."

With that comment, I knew who was calling. Kat's father. The Mafia boss.

I decided it would be best to play nice. "Good morning, Boris. Glad you called. Your daughter is next door in her own motorhome. By herself."

He laughed. "I know, I just talked to her. She filled me in on what happened and how you rescued her. She wouldn't tell me everything, and I suspect it's a lot more involved than what she said. But all that really matters is that she is safe. For that, I have you and Abby to thank. Probably mostly you."

I started to protest, to tell him it wasn't so much of a rescue as it was just tracking her down, but thought it better not to interrupt him. That would be rude.

He continued, "I want to repay you for your time, but I

know you won't take money. Last time you just gave it away. So I'm not going to give you cash. It'll be something though. You'll see.

He paused, then said, "Make sure she comes home safe. And speaking of safe, be careful around Abby. She's not always what she seems to be."

Before I could ask what he meant, he ended the call. That was probably a good thing since Abby was lying naked under the covers next to me. She had been sleeping until the phone rang. My conversation with Boris had woken her, and she wanted to know what he'd said.

I wasn't going to tell her everything, especially what he had said about her. But I let her know he was happy that Kat had been found safe and he appreciated what Abby had done to find her.

She smiled. "Why don't you lie back down? It's early, and maybe we could snuggle a bit."

Before I could answer, there was a knock on the door followed by, "I hope you two are up because we need to talk."

It was Kat, and she had a key.

While I was busy grabbing my shorts and shirt from the floor, Abby ran to the back bedroom where she'd undressed the night before.

When she was safely out of sight, I opened the door to see Kat standing there, a cup of coffee in hand.

She was smiling when she asked, "Anything going on in there that I should know about?"

I shook my head. "No, just sleeping in. Abby's in the back. Should I wake her?"

Kat nodded. "Yeah, get her up. We need to talk."

Instead of inviting her in, I told her I'd be right back and closed the door. She wouldn't like having it shut in her face, but it was better than her seeing Abby running around in her birthday suit.

I went to the back and tapped on the bedroom door. "You dressed?"

The door opened, and Abby peeked out. "Did you let her in?"

"No, she's waiting outside. She said we need to talk. All three of us."

Abby nodded. "You go on out there. Tell her I'll be out in a minute. Be sure to wear your ring."

I didn't know why she wanted me to wear the fake wedding ring. As far as I was concerned, finding Kat ended the 'pretending to be married' ruse.

But with Kat waiting outside, there wasn't time to talk about it, so I put the ring on and went out.

Kat noticed it right away, and asked, "You and Abby? Really?"

I shrugged. "It's complicated."

She nodded. "I guess it is. But let me warn you, be careful around her. She sometimes takes things a little too seriously."

I sensed Kat was about to tell me more, but she stopped when she saw the door open and Abby coming out.

She smiled and said, "Abby, you're looking good this morning. You must have had a good night."

Abby looked over at me and blushed. "Yeah, it was a good night. Just ask Walker."

Kat looked at me, shook her head and said, "You rascal. What have you two lovebirds been up to?"

Instead of answering, I changed the subject. "You said you needed to talk. What about?"

She smiled and pointed back to her motorhome. "I'm leaving today, headed over to the diamond mine in Murfreesboro. It's about an hour away and the state park there has a nice campground. Figured I could stay there for a day or two, look for diamonds and then go somewhere else. Maybe up into the mountains."

Camping at the diamond mine sounded like it might be fun, but I had a question. "What about the sheriff? Didn't he want you to stay put for a few days?"

She nodded. "Yeah, he did. But they called this morning and said they booked the fake deputy on murder charges and have enough evidence to guarantee a conviction.

"They said they won't be charging her with anything related to me or my motorhome. They said I was free to go. So I'm leaving. I've already packed up and plan to head out in an hour. What about you two? You sticking around?"

I didn't know what Abby's plans were, but I wanted to get back on the road. I wanted to head to Florida, drop her off and get on with what passed as normal life for me and Bob.

But Abby had a different plan. She put her arm around my waist and said, "They're holding the honeymoon suite for us at the Ameristar in Vicksburg. We'll be heading there later today."

Chapter Forty-Six

I definitely wanted to get back on the road and was pretty sure I needed to avoid the honeymoon suite. Abby's 'pretend we're married' ruse was starting to get a little weird.

I wanted to talk with Kat about it, since she'd known Abby a lot longer than I had, but Abby stuck close to me while I was around Kat, never giving us a chance to talk privately. I didn't know if she was doing this on purpose or if she just liked being around us.

In any case, I didn't get to talk to Kat about Abby before she left. After unhooking from shore power and checking the air in her tires, she hugged us both and said to call when we got back to Florida. Then she got in her motorhome and drove off.

As soon as she was out of sight, Abby turned to me and said, "How soon can we leave?"

I was glad to hear she was ready to get on the road, the sooner the better. I gave her the answer she wanted. "Twenty minutes. But we have to head back to Hot Springs to pick up your Jeep before we head to Florida."

Abby rubbed her hands with excitement and started singing, "I've got a Jeep; I've got a Jeep. I've got a little, green Jeep, Jeep, Jeep."

Twenty minutes later, we were on the road, heading back toward Daniel's shop where the Jeep was parked. Abby had called ahead to make sure it was ready. Grace answered and told her not only had they put the tow bar on it, they'd washed all the mud off it too.

When we got to the shop, the little Jeep was out front, and Daniel came out to help me hook it to the motorhome. We connected the tow bar and wiring harness, tested the brake and signal lights, and made sure it was ready to go. There were no problems; everything passed our inspection.

After thanking Grace and Daniel, Abby and I got back on the road and headed south, toward Florida, towing the Jeep behind us.

Five hours later, just as it was starting to get dark, we pulled into the Ameristar Casino campground. Abby went into the office and returned with the campsite card and a key.

"What's the key for?" I asked.

She smiled. "Remember back when we were in Hot Springs Village, when we saw Haley and her husband ride off in a golf cart? Remember what I said then?"

I remembered. "Something about us sitting side by side in a golf cart, riding off into the sunset."

She smiled and said, "Good memory. Anyway, this is the key to the golf cart the casino has given us to use during our stay. We can cruse the grounds, tour the riverfront, and maybe even ride off into the sunset in it."

I didn't bother to tell her we'd missed the sunset. No need to spoil her fun. Plus, I liked the idea of having a golf cart to get around the casino property. It sure beat hiking up the hill from the campground every time we wanted to get food.

After we got the motorhome parked and hooked up to shore power, I filled Bob's food and water bowl and let him know we'd be gone for a few hours. He didn't seem to mind. He probably looked forward to some 'alone time' after spending most of the previous evening with the three of us.

The two women and the box of wine made for a boisterous night, lots of laughs as they talked about old times.

I locked the motorhome, and we took the golf cart up to the casino. I drove and Abby sat close to me, a big smile on her face.

When we arrived at the main entrance, the valet took the cart and gave Abby a package from casino management. Inside were coupons for free meals, a hundred dollars in casino money and two card keys to the honeymoon suite.

I'd already decided I wasn't going up to the suite with her. She could sleep there if she wanted to, but I was going to sleep in the motorhome. I figured I would be safer there.

She sensed my reluctance and suggested we eat, spend a little time at the roulette wheels, and then decide where we'd spend the night. For me, my mind was already made up. I was going to sleep in my motorhome.

It wasn't that I didn't enjoy her company, because I did. It was just that I was getting the feeling that she was taking the 'pretend we're married' bit way too far. I didn't want to see her get hurt when we went our separate ways once we got back to Florida.

I tried to explain this to her over dinner, but she shrugged it off and said, "Don't worry about it. We're just having fun."

After that, I relaxed. We had a bottle of wine with our meal, spent an hour on the casino floor, and after Abby had won almost ten thousand dollars, we went to the honeymoon suite to 'catch a nap'.

The next morning, when I woke up in the suite's giant, heart-shaped bed, Abby was gone.

She'd left a note taped to the bathroom mirror that said, "It's been fun. GG."

I wasn't sure if the note meant she was gone, as in "Goodbye," or if she'd just gone down to get breakfast and would be back soon. I figured she was coming back, so I took a leisurely shower and cleaned up. I wanted to look my best when she returned.

When I got out of the shower, she still hadn't come back.

Thinking that maybe she had gone down to the casino and had lost track of time, I decided to go check. I pulled on my clothes and took the elevator down to the main floor and started looking for her. First stop, the roulette tables.

I checked the four different wheels, but there was no Abby. After that, I checked the other gaming areas and didn't find her at any of the tables or machines. Having struck out in the casino, I thought maybe she went back to the motorhome.

I crossed the casino floor and headed out the front door. When I saw the valet, I remembered the ticket we'd gotten the night before, pulled it out and asked, "Is the cart still available?"

He checked his board and came back with a key. "Yes sir, it is. I'm having it brought around for you."

A driver soon showed up with it and I tipped the valet and took it down the hill to where we'd parked the motorhome.

When I reached our site, I was happy to see it was still right where we'd parked it. I had given Abby a set of keys so she could come and go as needed and she could have used them to drive off in it, but she hadn't.

Before going in, I went around to the back to check on the Jeep.

It was gone. The tow bar had been unhooked from the motorhome and the Jeep had been driven away.

I was thinking it was probably Abby that took it, so I unlocked the motorhome and went in to see if she had left me a note. Bob met me at the door, sleepy eyed and grouchy. He looked behind me as I came in, wondering where my traveling companion was. I wondered the same thing.

Not seeing anyone following me in, Bob jumped up on the couch and huffed a groan of disappointment. He missed her. And so did I.

I checked the bedroom and saw that her clothes and suitcase were gone. The curtains she'd put up were still over the windows, but everything else of hers was missing.

I looked for a note but didn't find one. All I had were the few words she'd scribbled in the honeymoon suite. Apparently, she felt those were enough. "It's been fun. GG."

Not knowing whether she was coming back or not, I stayed in the casino campground another night. During the day, I tried to reach her on her phone but got no answer. After sending several texts, she finally texted back.

Her message said, "I'm safe. Had fun. We should do it again."

She signed it with, "Goat Girl."

Chapter Forty-Seven

The morning after she'd gone, as I was getting ready to head back to Florida, I found the extra set of keys I had given her. She'd put them on the driver's seat where she knew I couldn't miss them.

She'd left her fake wedding ring there as well. Something to remember her by.

I didn't take my ring off until I got back home. By then I'd spoken to Devin who had called to see how I was doing.

The first thing she said was, "I gave you three rules to follow. Don't let her drink. Don't let her gamble. And don't have sex with her.

"And what do you do? You go and break all three of them. You let her drink, you let her gamble, and you get her in bed. What exactly were you thinking, Walker?"

She continued, "I told you she was different. I told you to be careful around her. But no, you had to go and break the rules. Now you have to live with the consequences."

When she paused, I said, "Devin, what are you talking about? What did Abby tell you? What consequences?"

She laughed. "Walker, I'm just pulling your chain. I talked with her last night, and she said she had a great time. She said you had been a perfect gentleman and had treated her well.

"She said you even went along with her pretend marriage gag. But she was worried you might have taken it too seriously. She wanted me to call and let you down gently.

"She wants you to know she liked being with you, but she's not ready for a serious relationship with you or anyone else.

"She did say, if you could handle being around her without getting too attached, she would consider working with you again. In fact, she said Boris had a project in mind that would be perfect for the two of you.

"Something about lost treasure.

"Anyway, Abby wanted me to tell you she had a great time and if you want to work with her again, let her know."

Devin ended the call, giving me lots to think about.

Did I want to work with Abby again? And was I up for a treasure hunt?

The answer to both questions was yes. As soon as I got the invite, Bob and I would be ready to hit the road again in our motorhome.

Because life is too short to sit still.

Author's Notes

Most of the locations in this book are real, including the Coleman Crystal Mine in Jessieville, Arkansas and the RV park there. The Sweet Surrender mine and the Highway 27 Fish Village are also real places.

Even Crystal Mountain is real. In fact, the US Forest Service mentions Crystal Mountain in an old tour guide and provides a map to it in a publication titled, *Winona Auto Tour*. You can find the publication on the web at https://www.fs.usda.gov/Internet/FSE_DOCUMENTS/fsm9_039496.pdf

In that guide, they write:

"Not only does Crystal Mountain provide a scenic view of the surrounding National Forest, but it also offers the chance to collect what is considered to be the best quality quartz crystals in the world."

There is no mention of the Crystal Cave in the Forest Service guide, but it does exist. It's not easy to find, but it's there. I've been to it myself.

If you're tempted to go to Crystal Mountain, be careful. Don't go alone, don't go when the roads are wet, don't go at night and don't go during deer hunting season. Be aware of the presence of ticks, chiggers and snakes and take a four-wheel drive vehicle along with a Forest Service map of the area.

If you want to dig crystals without needing four-wheel

drive, check out Coleman's Crystal Mine in Jessieville, Arkansas, and the Sweet Surrender Mine in nearby Mt. Ida. Both are open to the public and are "keep all you find" mines.

While in the area, be sure to visit Hot Springs National Park, the historic bathhouses, and the local attractions.

Finally, if you like this book, please post a positive review on Amazon. Good reviews keep me motivated to create new volumes of the adventures of Mango Bob and Walker.

As always, thanks for your support.

Bill Myers

The adventure continues . . .

If you liked *Mango Digger*, please post a review at Amazon, and let your friends know about the Mango Bob series.

Other books in the Mango Bob series include:

Mango Bob

Mango Lucky

Mango Bay

Mango Glades

Mango Key

Mango Blues

You can find photos, maps, and more from the Mango Bob adventures at http://www.mangobob.com

Stay in touch with Mango Bob and Walker on Facebook at: https://www.facebook.com/MangoBob-197177127009774/

-

82260675R00178

Made in the USA
San Bernardino, CA
14 July 2018